S A T O R
A R E P O
T E N E T
O P E R A
R O T A S

James — So glad to have found you in S.F., thanks for all your love.

Confessions from a Dark Wood

by

~~Eric Raymond~~

Eric Raymond

Published by Sator Press
First Edition
2012

ISBN 978-0-9832437-1-7
Library of Congress Control Number:
2012940212

cover design by Ken Baumann
text set in Fournier

SatorPress.com
Los Angeles, CA

Confessions from a Dark Wood

The Secret Lives of
C-Suite Consultants
in the Post-Idea Economy

by

Eric Raymond with Nick Bray

Advance Praise for *Confessions from a Dark Wood:*

"We are thrilled to review Raymond's rich and nuanced chronicle of Nick Bray's immersion into the multifaceted language of our post-idea economy. Through Nick's pioneering eyes, we see how the formerly protected frontiers of marketplace innovation are not only mapped in color for the first time, but exhaustively strip-mined and clear-cut for the enrichment of business minds scattered across the truly biggest generation. This is a deep intellectual dive by Raymond and Bray, and I am profoundly grateful to receive a gift like this in my lifetime."

—Pontius J. LaBar, CEO, LaBar Partners Limited

"In a Web 2.0 universe, where the traditional silos of corporate identities collide and reinvent themselves with new strains of story-driven DNA and a myriad of cross-platform data matrices, it is imperative we create new models for interpreting Bray's voice. Contextual issues redefine the definers. Following Bray's linguistic breadcrumbs requires we not only trace the same path deep into his dark woods, but when in the witch's kitchen, learn the consumer-co-created interfaces for temperature adjustment and seasoning, and therefore taste, first-hand, the unique culinary outcomes."

—Randi Bevelecazzo, SVP of Liquid Content & Evolving Brand Ecosystems, LaBar Partners Limited

"Go viral?"

—Chet Wallace, VP of Client Strategy, LaBar Partners Limited

"Apt."

—Senior Executive (Anon.), Canard Consulting International

"That's a lot of motherfucking words, know what I'm saying? Like, hundreds. Shit. Could be *thousands*. My boy Slim Jim is deep, feel me?"

—Shaun D. Braun, Client, Ex-NFL running back & One True Commissioner ("Tha O.T.C.") of the FNDFL (First National Dog Fighting League)

"I am currently out of the office with limited access to email. Your message is very important to me, however, and I will attend to it as soon as I am able, in the order it was received. If you have immediate concerns over the whereabouts of a loved one, I assure you they are receiving the full extent of the personalized services for which they paid."

—Mr. Z, Client, Chief Operative, Rendition Vacations, L.L.C.

"Oh please help… *[unintelligible]* Please! Help… *[wet / unintelligible]* No! Don't! No! This isn't—ah— *[unintelligible]*! Stop it! No! Stop!"

—Intern (of the Salmon Shirt), LaBar Partners Limited

"*[Mournful hoot.]*"

—Shelby the Orangutan, Special Executive Advisor, LaBar Partners Limited

"I'll be damned."

—Jacob Jude Hawkins, *Yale Younger Poets Series Award Winner*, TSA Screener, Passenger Carry-on Luggage, San Francisco International Airport

"I told you they wouldn't read it first."

—Nick Bray, ex-VP, LaBar Partners Limited, Narrator

"Oh, so you finally have a book. You must be proud. Congratulations, son. You know, in the afterlife, books are our toilet paper. I'm saying we literally wipe our asses with books. Go figure."

—Dr. Michael W. Bray (Deceased), Ph.D., Dept. of English, Endowed Chair of Cervantes Studies, St. John's Landing University

Author's Foreword

This book is a work of fiction. Names, characters, places, and incidents either are products of the author's imagination or are used fictitiously. Any resemblance to actual events or locales or persons, living or dead, is coincidental. This work is intended solely as an entertaining diversion.

No actual Porsches were harmed in the making of this book.

Narrator's Foreword

What I went through, and what appears here, is, if anything, a botched attempt at non-fiction. You may think it reads as my absurd and ill-conceived nightmare, stained with hyperbole and the grotesque, but it doesn't go far enough.

I assure you that despite strenuous verisimilitude, this book falls short of the bare-ass insanity, the perversion of intellectual capital, and the pernicious and epidemic squandering of promising human energy, which is, in turn, directly responsible for the steady undermining of America.

A staggering amount of money reinforces this.

My few seasons touring the country with LaBar Partners Limited is a corner of the bigger picture, which if you are able step back, will reveal more than our common spiritual desolation, but a holistic retreat from logic, compassion, and meaning.

(Jesus, I *still* sound like I'm writing proposals.)

And the Devil finally says to Bobby Gould, "You're a very bad man." And Bobby Gould says, "Nothing's black and white." And the Devil says, "Nothing's black and white, nothing's black and white—what about a panda? What about a panda, you dumb fuck! What about a fucking panda!"

David Mamet, The Art of the Theater No. 11, *The Paris Review*, No. 142 (Spring, 1997)

For my father

1946 - 2007

Executive Summary

Chapter One

In Which Nick Bray is Peremptorily Recruited by LaBar Partners Limited

When I was 33, I consulted in a dark wood.

I didn't know at the time that the edge of that dark wood was the sunny, sweaty veranda of the President's mansion at St. John's Landing University, where my father taught literature for thirty-six years. I was merely back again in the small Florida town where I was raised, attending my father's funeral, acting in the way of people who do not yet know they are lost. I had moved to San Francisco three years prior, but I made occasional trips home under the duress of my mother's coaxing and periodic legal obligation (see also: young marriage and divorce; pending home sale; division of assets).

I owned no suit, so I mingled with the university crowd wearing a white Cuban shirt, jeans, and a brown pair of broken down, slip-on Kenneth Cole's. Someone who's face I can't recall said *Nice of you to dress up*, which passed through me without making a mark, as so much did that day. I was both elated and annihilated; on one hand, the thing I had feared since I was nine years old had come to pass, and so now it couldn't happen again. On the other, the thing I had feared since I was nine years old was actually happening.

If Faulkner had access to anti-depressants, the university President's mansion would have graced the cover of *Absalom! Absalom! The Musical.* Though strip malls ground out the live oaks up and down most of St. John's thoroughfares, the mansion docked against the university like a Hollywood icon of the prelapsarian South. White columns, green lawn, wrought iron, decorative shutters. The jasmine crawled up, the Spanish moss reached down. University faculty, students, locals, friends, second and third ring relations with honorary Uncle and Aunt titles, and even some lost strangers touring the campus for the first time washed up on the memorial veranda.

My father had left no specific instructions regarding a funeral, so it was left up to my mother. I suppose she had mentally prepared for this in so many different stages of their 39-year marriage, that when the time came, the energy to carry-off the actual memorial service had long unspooled with universal laws of entropy. It looked like a church yard sale.

Mourners ascended a short flight of steps to reach the veranda, and then entered a kind of slaughterhouse track of low, rectangular folding tables covered in paper tablecloths. One one side, a buffet of foods that would have caused my father's cardiologists and endocrinologists to blanche. On the other, the tables were littered with artifacts of my father's life. Owing to my recent five hour flight, it reminded me a little of photographs of NTSB warehouses where they gather up all of the fragments of a commercial air disaster.

Assembled were family photographs, an imitation Cubs uniform jersey I gave him for his 50th birthday, soft-back copies of his few published books, an algae-grimed orange tackle box filled with rust-dusted lures and rainbow plastic worms, assorted caricatures given as gifts from department secretaries, a prehistoric wooden tennis racquet, poker chips stacked beside a spade straight flush (sans royalty), and finally, because Dr. Michael W. Bray was a Cervantes scholar, an entire section crowded with a rag-tag army of Don Quixote and Sancho Panza figurines, peppered with windmills, attended to by both sag-backed, bony-rumped Rocinantes as well as their imaginary Romance counterparts in full battle dress.

An unplanned mix of my father's favorite music from his youth competed with the human din, and the Beatles' *All You Need is Love* bumped against The Stones' *Mother's Little Helper*. An extra table, entirely empty, stood at the end of the line, its purpose unclear. Maybe it was for dirty dishes, or the socket for a petty cash box at this final garage sale. It might have stood for all that was omitted from a memorial, i.e. a few decades of filching undergraduate panties, a pyramid of Miller Lite cans, a tape loop of doors slamming around our house, and the amputated legs below the knee, which had shuffled off this mortal coil six years ahead of my father.

The bolt through the brain at the end of line was the double-life-sized portrait of Dr. Michael W. Bray in black and white, a shot of him behind the classroom podium, dominated by his head in its full-haired and scrub-brush eyebrow mania. It was snapped in an era of continuous fear of death and the height of health, when he carried a tweedy sport coat over extra forty pounds on two healthy legs, and his single snaggling canine pinched his lower lip when he grinned. This bygone image of Dr. Bray leaned in the blue pleather seat of his constant companion, a cut-rate Lumex manual wheelchair, creating the effect that now they had finally amputated everything, save the memory of him in his chalk-throwing, wick-dipping, hard-playing heyday.

I stood in front of his portrait, straining on some level to imagine what it was he would have to say to me now, when someone touched me on the elbow.

"Excuse me, are you Nick Bray?"

The kid looked like a fit, frattish undergraduate, blonde and perhaps a little short, and twitched haltingly when he spoke, as you might expect of a bag man at a heavily surveilled ransoming.

"I'm Nick."

He swallowed. His eyelids fluttered as he spooled up a memorized speech.

"I'm here to inform you Mr. LaBar sends his deepest condolences. He is absolutely distraught."

It took me a moment to place the name. Of course I had heard of him from my father. Pontius J. LaBar. "P.J." in our family circle. Much later I would have instantly recognized the kid's teal, $175 Thomas Pink shirt with the monogrammed cuff as the mark of a mid-list Intern at LaBar Partners Limited.

"*P.J.* LaBar?"

"*Mr.* LaBar. Yes."

I looked around. "Is he here?"

"Well, ah, no," he cleared his throat. "I'm here *for* him. On his behalf." He smiled broadly.

"Ok. I guess… thank you?"

"I assure you, he very much regrets he is engaged at the executive level today."

It took me a moment to understand what he had said, and it seemed that I was expected to say something back, though the longer we stared at one another, the more I felt like the rookie in the espionage film missing my half of the secret pass phrases.

"I'll be sure to tell my mother that P.J. sent you… as his… regards."

"Additionally," the Intern said, "I've been asked to request your presence at Mr. LaBar's headquarters in Atlanta to discuss the possibility of your joining the firm."

"I live in San Francisco."

"Naturally Mr. LaBar will fly you to Atlanta for the meeting."

I should have known then how much travel would be required. The Intern produced a small ivory envelope in heavy stock and extended it my way. My name was quilled in black ink on the front, and on the reverse side, across an orange wax seal, spanned the raised silhouette of a giraffe. How I would come to loathe that logo.

The Intern lowered his head. I thought if I didn't take the envelope I would be violating one of those unwritten customs of another country, as when one inadvertently points a bare foot in the direction of the host and is dragged from his bed that night and lashed within an inch of his life. Yet I was tempted to not take it anyhow, just to see if the Intern would die on the spot.

The Intern glowered and spoke quietly: "You should consider it, Mr. Bray."

"I should?"

He nodded. "Strongly."

"You tell me, you work for him—"

The thought pleased him and embarrassed him so much that the little rain cloud on his head blew away. "Oh, no, no," the Intern shook his head, grinning a million *aw-shucks* a minute. "Maybe *one day*. If I'm lucky. I'm just interning."

In a sequence of surreal events—the sudden death of your father, a call in the middle of the night, a cross-country flight in which they mix advertising with safety instructions, and the vertigo of a few hundred mourners milling through a memorial flea market—one more surreal event doesn't even register. When Alice drank the potion and started shrinking, she wasn't about to say, *Hold on, talking rabbits? Are you fucking kidding me?* One hit and she was all in.

I didn't ask why anyone thought I'd be worth hiring for a job I didn't know existed. I would have probably tucked the card in my back pocket and forgotten about it entirely, but the Intern summoned up the five whispered words that undid me:

"You will be well compensated."

Magic.

I took the card. The Intern let loose an exhalation of relief. Without another word he descended the back stairs of the veranda, mincing between a damp clutch from the philosophy department primarily engaged in a potato salad dialectic. He crossed the back lawn to the sandy vacant lot which served as the mansion's guest parking, fumbling with his keys. He'd sweated straight through the back of his shirt.

I looked back at the portrait of my father, his lecture eternally suspended.

I turned to look again when I heard the unmistakable roar of a sports car. A pugnacious gunmetal Porsche Carerra Twin Turbo with tinted windows sped beyond the hedges adjacent to the parking lot. Trailing behind was the Intern in an undistinguished white rental sedan, balancing a video camera on the dash with one hand.

At the corner, a pedestrian stepped from the curb, and the Porsche railed on its horn. It gunned around the stunned old man at the last moment, fishtailing across the main boulevard. The Intern's car lagged behind, but not for long. He ran the stop sign and soon they were gone from view.

It didn't cross my mind at the time, but of course it had been P.J. LaBar's car the Intern followed. I later learned he was not just following LaBar, but also acting as his *chase camera*.

The problem, from P.J.'s point of view, was that you could not drive behind the Porsche you were currently driving, and you were therefore robbed of the very experience that sold you the car in the first place—the salacious visual feast of its humps and rump racing around. He was indignant that his six-figure image was squandered unjustly on the soccer mom in the Toyota Sienna and her five-year-old, grinding a mortar of drool and Cheerios into the grimy fabric seats.

His personal solution for this problem was to have Interns film him as he drove (which was admittedly not often, the Porsche was pretty tight inside), so that he could *maximize the pleasure return on his luxury-performance brand investment.* He became so entranced with this idea for a spell that it was reported by others in the firm that he had gone as far to have a lavish proposal drafted for Porsche's consideration; they could offer a premium chase camera service to high-end clients. Something involving off-duty cab drivers and a partnership with Canon. Astonishingly, he got a meeting, but Porsche did not call back for a second.

These are but a handful of several thousand details I am trying to forget.

I went into this whole thing blind. All I really knew of Pontius J. LaBar and his shadowy LaBar Partners Limited was the fragmentary history provided by my father, who had been P.J.'s academic advisor at St. John's University. A baffled and bright undergraduate searching for an identity. A professor who flipped some switch in the kid's head. A period in the business-end of the wilderness in which the college graduate is nurtured by wolves, who he then kills and eats. The young wolf becomes boy CEO, the old professor safely stored away in his inconvenient history. Many millions of dollars pass in an Orson Welles calendar montage. The eponymous firm ascends rapidly, producing nothing but the myth of itself.

I left the memorial midway through and walked across campus to my father's office on the basement floor of Davis Hall with its coronial air conditioning. Among the Xanax in my pocket I found the spare key from my mother. Wedged in the cracks around the door were a few notes from his current students. I collected them. On the floor inside lay a late and hasty term paper with a long plea for leniency, its hungover author still unaware that Dr. Michael Bray had retired his red pen two days ago.

I kept the lights off. The sun bled through the canted blinds, and the office swam with dust in a monochrome blue. Half of my father's books were packed in boxes, their margins filled with the cramped and cryptic handwriting which fueled hours of lectures. I had it in mind that I would ship the boxes back to San Francisco, though I had no plans for them. Newer shelves in a smaller, shittier room 3,000 miles away. An academic fate.

I packed books. Dream songs and motorcycle maintenance and the mirror and the lamp. I discovered a dusty bourbon bottle in his file cabinet's bottom drawer. I stopped packing books. I settled in the low chair before the receiving end of his desk, my old catcher's position for Dr. Bray's pitches on how I'd been mismanaging my life. An index of my undones, unfinisheds, and unrealizeds in alphabetical order. Admonition from above when I rappelled from the ivory tower.

After a fresh pour, I picked up my chair and positioned it on the other side of his desk, in the vacancy of his handicap parking space.

He do fatherly advice in different voices.

I'd never been to a cremation before.

There was that to look forward to.

Chapter Two

In Which Nick Bray Performs a Rapid & Frank Accounting of His Living Conditions, Career Path, & Meets a Special Friend

On approach at San Francisco International, the jets are vectored in such a way that they cross the yellow halogen pearls of the San Mateo bridge and descend gradually towards the Bay. Passengers who have never experienced this approach often murmur with increasing alarm as the 767-200 appears to be deliberately easing into a freezing bath at a ground speed of one hundred and fifty seven miles an hour. At the last possible moment, a marshy gravel appears, and then the safe-home scorched border of runway 28R.

Depending on my mood, I occasionally imagined what it would be like to catch, out of the corner of my eye, the shape of a black boat bobbing where it shouldn't be, its running lights dark. The flash is like a spark from an outlet, and the shoulder-fired rocket sweeps up to meet us before we touchdown.

My friend Jake Hawkins tells me that this is unlikely. He tells me that a veteran pilot with a cool head and a little luck would be able to put the jet down in one piece despite a rocket hit on approach. He says they're much more likely to concentrate a dual rocket attack on take-off, when the wings are fat with fuel. But then again, he's a poet and a baggage screener at SFO. So, grain of salt.

He reminds me there are death fantasies that do not involve acts of terrorism.

Not anymore, I tell him.

Thirty-six thousand feet above the Grand Canyon and pointing west, I read a full-page advertorial in SkyMall Magazine on a NASA-inspired diaper harness for dogs. This canine poop carry-on redistributed the indignity of scooping up hot piles of shit in plastic bags. The filter bags for the harness were lined with *100% compostable, environmentally friendly organic odor neutralizers. Now your dog can become an active participant in the greening of America, and a family contributor to your community garden's summer tomato patch.*

Someone at SkyMall knew exactly where this plane was landing.

Welcome to the Bay Area.

I loved San Francisco when I had a little money in my pocket. But without at least a little, I spent a lot of sour time observing how the Mexican guys stacked flat cardboard boxes nine feet high in the back of their graffiti bright pickup while up the block a guy parallel parked his Maserati. Sure, any city was this way, but in the ramshackle movie set of San Francisco, there wasn't enough room to keep disparities at dignified distances.

Flying left me punchy and bone tired. Speeding underground between Mission & 16th and Mission & 24th, the BART train deafened passengers with a banshee howl and threatened all of us with imminent disintegration. At Civic Center the MUNI trains were locked in a staring contest with one another. A kid in a hoodie talked incessantly into his cell phone about how he was going to move back to New York. A lot of people were going back to New York, they just had to make sure everyone in San Francisco heard about it first.

I abandoned the trains and busses and walked up Market toward home in the Western Addition. (NOPA is a restaurant, the Western Addition is a neighborhood.) Pious car choices nested like Russian dolls. A Prius, a Mini Cooper, and a Smart Car walk into a bar.

Sprayed across a plywood wall protecting the open pit which would become a new high-rise in Hayes Valley, a graffiti kid had stenciled a skeletal horse vomiting blood. The blood spelled: *GOD GAVE NEWSOM THE RAINBOW SIGN! NO MORE WATER! GENTRI-FIRE NEXT TIME!*

Our heavy sow of a house stood out as the cannibalized rental on the block, with its peeling paint and black plastic garbage sack permanently duct-taped in the widow's peak attic window. I split the second floor of the toothless old swine of a Victorian on Hayes with three other people and a Great Dane-Labrador mutt named Sagamore. Home again, I spilled my duffel bag on the bed. It smelled like my mother's house.

I seldom saw my roommates. Russ tended bar two blocks away and rarely showed up until three in the morning. Occasionally we would go on a bender and drink free with all of the other bartenders on shift who came in while Russ was working, and they were off. The first secret to surviving the city's high cost of living was settling for a quarter of America's median living standard. The second secret to surviving the city's high cost of living? Create a network of friends in the service industry.

My next roommate was a reedy kid named Petey, with full sleeve tattoos and a wild style mural inked earlobe to earlobe. He had escaped New Jersey, spoke of it like three tours in Vietnam, and worked in the Mission at an artisan irony store where they sold Hamm's Beer, toasted and microwaved Velveeta and bacon sandwiches on Wonderbread, and sold "superfixie" bikes with wheels that did not turn.

I do not mean these bikes lacked a freewheel. I mean the wheels were literally tack welded in place. The thing to do was hang them on the wall or sit on them near Dolores Park when you weren't carrying them on your shoulder. This was a relatively new subculture war, and since I've wondered if it wasn't the experiment of a hipster mockumentary or Urban Outfitters market research project. Petey's job, as he described it to me once, smoking on our front steps, was to sound like he was from New Jersey, drink Hamm's, and strenuously ignore people. Sagamore was Petey's sandblasted dog, and so named because of a degenerative muscle condition which affected his head, causing the skin under his eyes and around his snout to hang like a stroke victim's. He had once been named "Champion."

Proof the last roommate even existed came only from the periodic appearance of a low light under his door and the occasional calypso rhythm and spring moan of his bed frame thrashing the wall. Having paid cash outright for a year's worth of rent, he received no mail, and was rumored to be called either Marcus or Brent, depending on who I talked with (Russ called him Brent, Petey called him Marcus). He was the best roommate you could hope for, assuming the severed head of a woman didn't appear in the freezer one weekend. I put him on being a wealthy married guy from Marin who slummed in Western Addition bars for USF girls or boys, though Russ had never seen him out. Our unspoken agreement was not to pry, as his occupation of the largest room in the house kept the rest of our rents under $600 a piece.

Money matters loomed.

At the time of my father's death, I temped at an internet porn company named *Purv* which specialized in the niche of industrial machine porn. They were the masters of mechanized fucking, the doctors of advanced dildonics, the mad laboratory of steampunked sex and electrostim labia clipping. Connoisseurs of *Purv's* niche preferred zero male participation, and the girls were post-punk, vampire gothy, or wholesome farm girls with a thing for the combine. They enjoyed full health care benefits with no deductible, 100% match 401ks, and access to subsidized housing in *Purv's* studio lofts four blocks away, provided they passed semi-regular drug tests and showed up when they said they would. I had heard that early on *Purv* offered fractional ownership in the videos, which meant that the girls pocketed a small royalty each time the content was resold. Save the camera crew, everyone else was temp or part-time, sans benefits.

The building *Purv* purchased was south of Market Street in a foreboding ex-armory which still bore the black-and-yellow signs labeled FALLOUT SHELTER. The ground floor housed the reception area and a phalanx of typical tech-company cubicles and offices, connected in the back to a spacious machine shop. The top floors were post-production, web development, affiliate and web traffic management, accounting, technical support, and a dot-commish rec room packed with all of the amenities that flowed down Howard and Bryant at six cents on the dollar when the vaporware companies tanked. A freight elevator connected the machine shop to the studios below street level. Once in a while, you would see a new girl sitting in the reception area for an interview, but the working actresses steered clear of the upper floors, where our bored army spent most of their days processing hardcore images or dealing with the mundane cash flow details surrounding *Purv's* enormous profits.

Purv's founders still took an active interest in the business, being *passionistas* themselves for the unity of woman and machine. Ray Vance was an old hippie machinist from Fresno and his partner, Collin Baker, was a Stanford MBA and tech startup burnout. They were frequently in the machine shop together, among the partially-assembled pneumatic pumps and small tool engines, fiddling with robotics and silicone molds, while the production assistants ran racks of the "business end" parts from the day's shoots through commercial dishwashers and autoclaves.

It smelled of acetylene and industrial lubricants and popcorn, as

Ray Vance had an insatiable appetite for the buttery stuff, and kept a full-scale movie theatre popcorn machine stocked and running all day long. On last pass, an old-school chalk board displayed a sketch for what looked like a motorized wheelchair fitted with a black horse saddle and gynecologists stirrups. In the open lot behind the machine shop, a circle of wooden picnic tables allowed for lunch outside if you weren't of a mind to sit in the coffin-plush rec room, which I often did. Short on cash, I was on the one-burrito-a-day diet. Coffee for breakfast, half a burrito for lunch, the other half for dinner. Ray Vance spotted me a bag of popcorn for my walk home.

My specific job consisted of finalizing and uploading the videos to *Purv's* websites, writing some of the video descriptions, and editing and partially censoring video stills for the teaser pages. Thankfully, we were all required to wear headphones, or else the top floor would have sounded like a great sapphic polyphonic orgy in a Detroit auto assembly line. After a couple of weeks, complete porn desensitization set in, and I barely registered what was going on in the videos. I was, however, increasingly perplexed by how to wittily describe, for the nine hundredth time, the intersection of Black & Decker, synthetic appendages, and wax-bald vaginas. The cubicle I inherited was peppered with cheat-sheets of nouns, verbs, and adjectives tacked up behind the monitor to make the copywriting easier.

A web page on the *Purv* intranet helped the temp web monkeys like myself keep the machine names straight. It showed each machine with a brief video clip, so that we would never accidentally disappoint our loyal following by calling a machine by the wrong name. We were reminded constantly to refer to it. In a company-wide email one morning, Collin Baker underscored the importance of accuracy by sharing a "not uncommon" customer service email.

The message customer service received was from 36-month member ($1,078.20) "BigOleBoi," (Don Lemmon, 39-year-old regional bank manager in Tulsa, Oklahoma) calling attention to the fact that in video #278 ("Go On Down on the Funny Farm") we had misrepresented "Licksaw's" top-tongue speed at 3,000 CHM (clit-hits-per minute), when in video #112, ("Lumberjackin' Time") Licksaw's control dial clearly indicated a maximum upper limit of 4,500 CHM. *Could we please clear up this discrepancy?*

BigOleBoi was not alone in his attention to detail—the *Purv* forums were jammed with fans who carried the stats of the sex machines in their heads the way others knew the earned run and batting averages of major league ball players. The most active thread on the forum was one in which members regularly discussed what types of future robots could be added to the *Purv* family. Other members collaborated online over long, meticulous scripts for Ray Vance and Collin Baker to shoot. When Collin Baker once picked up the idea of issuing gasoline-scented limited edition collector's cards, modeled after Topp's baseball cards, the entire run of 500 sold out at $89.95 each. Rumor had it plans were underway for a massive live event to take place in an old Air Force hangar in Nevada, a project the members referred to as "Yearning Man."

So when I returned from Florida, head fogged in and body beat to hell by five hours in a center seat on Southwest, I accidentally made the mistake of labeling the robot in a new scene "Captain Fucktronic" when it was actually "The Dildonator." The mistake generated nearly three hundred flaming all-caps or all-lowercase emails in the customer service department, two cubes to my right. It did not help matters that Captain Fucktronic and The Dildonator were major rivals in our continuing sci-fi miniseries, *Warpdriver*.

Word reached the machine shop an hour later, and Collin Baker rounded up the entire support staff in the rec room for an emergency meeting. We filed in to find Ray Vance sitting in his oversized, stuffed purple chair, a prop ripped straight from a Dr. Seuss book. He looked dejected. Bits of popcorn nestled in his long salt and pepper beard. Collin Baker waited until the room was full and then stormed in for maximum dramatic effect, his shirtsleeves cuffed by equal centimeters to the elbows.

Though both Vance and Baker had a genuine enthusiasm for *Purv's* content, it's worth noting that Ray Vance saw the enterprise as a labor of love and Collin Baker's heart was closer to his wallet. Collin's assistant dimmed the lights. An LCD projector descended from the ceiling. Collin stood beside Ray Vance, sad porn robot king, and pointed a remote at the laptop connected to the projector. A bright image of Captain Fucktronic and all of his weaponized appendages filled the wall.

"People," Collin began, "who is this?"

"Captain Fucktronic," we said in a dim, asynchronous chorus. Ray Vance turned his head and looked at the screen lovingly. The PowerPoint slide advanced. An action shot of The Dildonator appeared.

"Very good. Now who is this?"

"The Dildonator," we said, a little more with it.

"Wow, hey, that's right. Gosh. It's hard to understand how we managed to fuck up so bad today, seeing how you all clearly can tell the difference between the two." Collin advanced the slide and both robots appeared side by side. "Just in case *someone* out there is not quite clear, let me point out a few of the more obvious differences." Collin waved his laser pointer over the two robots in shaky circles. "Here? And here? Here? See?"

We murmured assent.

"Let me express this clearly: If anyone still doesn't get it, we can arrange for a free first-hand experience with the two. I *assure you* the differences will be *vivid*."

The room was silent. Ray Vance sighed heavily.

"It just bums me out, man," he said in a low voice. "These are like... my kids."

Collin nodded vigorously.

"You know who else it bums out?" Collin picked up. "*Our paying members!* You know, the ones with the credit cards?" The lights brightened and Collin closed his laptop with a snap.

His body language softened, he hung his head like a disappointed father and squeezed Ray's shoulder reassuringly.

"Folks, never forget this: We are storytellers. This enterprise of ours—it's about creating and maintaining the unbroken arc of a fantastic, magical ream. When we make mistakes, even smaller ones than this, the inconsistencies destroy the fantasy for our fans, and they are rudely blue balled by our sloppiness."

Two months hence, I would more or less hear the same speech from Pontius J. LaBar's mouth in the boardroom of a Fortune 500 company.

"This isn't 1999. We're not the only machine erotica shop in the game any more. Members have choices. We may be the first and the best, but we're only the best because we're customer service fanatics. Do I need to rent Tony Hsieh for an hour to cheer you fuckers up? Attention to detail, people. When we fail to uphold the high standards, members notice, and we lose market share."

"I remember the day they were born." Ray Vance rescued an edible kernel in his beard and consoled himself.

Collin Baker met each of our eyes, hands on hips. "You want to go through the motions, start filling out your apps for Starbucks. Dismissed."

We began our penguin waddle out. The idea of free coffee and working with fully clothed women in aprons was by this time far more arousing than another eight hours pixelating nipples a-la alligator clips.

Then: "Nick, can we talk with you for a minute?"

It was as if they read my thoughts.

Ray Vance and Collin Baker freed me up to explore my barista options the very same day.

You have not been thoroughly blacklisted from temporary employment until your agency finds out you were shit-canned from a porn company. They'd been notified prior to the meeting and hung up on me when I called to request a new assignment. A guy with biceps like grapefruits escorted me to the receptionist's front desk. I remembered my half-eaten burrito in the rec-room fridge. Since I didn't think Ray Vance would come charging out with a fare-thee-well bag of popcorn, I couldn't leave the burrito behind. I pleaded with the security guy and he reluctantly disappeared back upstairs to fetch it for me.

This was when I met Sadie Parrish.

She was a loose limbed, straight red-haired beauty with a cosmic calm and twee librarian's glasses above a bridge of light freckles. On her lap a copy of *Circuit Cellar* lay open. Her lips moved slightly as she read. I was instantly smitten.

I blurted "You don't want to work here."

She looked up and took me in. She squinted at me through her glasses. Her attention was like being shot to death with spring sunshine.

"How do you know where I want to work?" She closed her magazine.

"I don't know where you *want* to work, but I know where you *don't* want to work. And that would be here."

She closed her magazine. "Sounds like you might have a little problem with female empowerment, huh?"

"Are you kidding? Tell me you're kidding."

"Why would I be kidding?"

"Let me see if I can put it another way: When was the last time you were double-penetrated by twin eight-inch dildos driven by a six-speed Chevy transmission?"

When she looked away and laughed, I noticed the Apple logo tattooed on the back of her neck.

"Is that how you ask all the girls out for coffee?"

"Did I ask you to coffee?"

"Maybe I asked me for you."

"And what did you say?"

"I said yes."

"That's pretty unusual."

She opened her magazine again.

"I'm glad you asked. Your afternoon should be as free as mine."

"I'm not walking out on this interview. If you have all this new free time, wait for me."

"You should skip the interview. They won't hire you with that tattoo on your neck. No logos, trademarks, or rights-managed characters or likenesses on the actresses. If you had one of those trashy tribal wingdings, no problem. But no logos. Post production would go out of their mind tracking and blurring it, and it would ruin it for the members anyway. Thing is, they won't tell you that until after you've auditioned, know what I mean?"

She bit her bottom lip and seemed genuinely deflated.

"Fucked before I was fucked."

"Way of the world."

The security guard came back with my burrito and stood by the receptionist's desk to see me out. Sadie looked as though she understood.

"Alrighty then," the security guy said. "Time to go." He held the burrito at arm's length like a full diaper. I took it.

He held the door for me, a gesture of civility I owed to Sadie's presence, I was sure. I stepped outside into the afternoon wind. She wasn't standing yet, but she leaned over to look at me through the open door.

"Soooo… I guess it's coffee o'clock," she said.

I felt like I had to shout as the traffic crowded past.

"I can't afford to buy you a cup of coffee. But I can offer you half of a burrito." I waggled my foil package in the air. She stood up and rolled her magazine as if to scold a dog. She stepped outside into that cold and descending light. The security guard shut the door, and we were among the homeless and the windblown garbage.

"What if I loan you a cup of coffee?"

"That's sort of a relief. It was my last half burrito."

"Please, please shut up. You had me at double penetration."

Once in your life should you be so lucky to meet someone like this. Meet someone you start with in media res. Meet someone who seems as though they've known you for who you are your entire life. Meet someone improbably, and understand every meaningless moment guided you to this high-speed collision.

The 49 Mission-Van Ness bus lumbered up from the curb and left us there with a poorly understood but shared secret. The fog crushed over the hills above South San Francisco. Take it all as a gift if it comes to you like this.

I would offer one caveat, however: Before it comes, as Sadie Parrish appeared to me in *Purv's* lobby, file a small prayer that the girl you meet has no ambitions to become the country's first domestic suicide bomber. Because Sadie did, and who was I to dissuade her from a life's ambition?

Her older brother, Staff Sergeant Anthony Parrish, had been killed in Afghanistan, and the shockwave from his roadside bomb traveled all the way across the world and sheared her family into pieces. She was twenty-two and done with the yellow ribbons and oak trees. She didn't tell me this the day I was fired from *Purv*. When a fresh tattoo of the Starbucks logo appeared on her stomach after one of my two week stints on the road, we had a talk.

But that day of loaned coffee: I tramped home late, buzzing with the day, the reality of my financial situation settled on my shoulders. Little money remained. I could not subdivide my burrito into smaller and smaller sustaining portions. Laundry called. I batted the mound of clothes around, looking for jeans with spare cash tucked away, happy-hour style. I found none, but I did discover the invitation from LaBar Partners Limited crumpled at the bottom of my army green duffel. I sat alone on the edge of my bed and turned the unopened invitation in my hand.

Sometimes the runway appears at the last second.

Chapter Three

A Recollection of Nick's First Visit to the Headquarters of LaBar Partners Limited

How far away that first limo ride to the airport seems now, arranged on my behalf. How quickly I became used to it. How soft and cold the deep back seats of the devil's chauffeured Lincoln Continental, how exotic his brands of bottled water and juice in the passenger's center console. How solicitous the driver in servitude at 4:45 AM, how crisp and warm his copies of the *Wall Street Journal* and *New York Times*. How strange to have these new words fastened to your boarding group: *Prèmiere. Platinum Medallion. Red Carpet.* How the smoked glass parts for you like biblical seas and opens unto business lounges appointed like the fresh tombs of pharaohs. How obsidian your AMEX and how sharp its edge as it cuts through desk clerks and hostesses and concierges and resistance. How there is the wine list behind the wine list and then the very short handwritten one the sommelier keeps against his own heart.

The offices of LaBar Partners Limited occupied the top four floors of the Peachtree Plaza Towers on Peachtree St. NW near Midtown Atlanta. Atlanta used the word "Peachtree" like a four-year-old with a new swear word. The area was crowded with the modern buildings of Georgia Tech and beige commerce, towering over and shouldering older structures as if impatiently waiting for them to pass away. Several blocks off, across from the historic Fox Theater and a clutch of burned-out and urine-extinguished storefronts, rose the Grand Atlantan Terrace Hotel where I stayed when in Atlanta. It was a former county fair beauty queen run to fat and wrapped in a magnolia printed muumuu, adamantly refusing to acknowledge the passage of fifty years. It was telling that the closer I was to the LaBar tower, the more shabby my accommodations. There were no luxury hotels within walking distance of the office.

I was given instructions at check-in to proceed directly to the executive offices of the Peachtree Plaza Towers.

For a company with four floors leased on the tallest building in Midtown, the executive offices were uncommonly quiet. I passed through the glass double doors, etched with the twin profiles of giraffes, immediately into a lavish but ghostly reception area in white. It resembled a studiously neutered and staged urban condominium, filled with similar, but not precisely matching modern furniture, and ornate patterned rugs over laminate imitation hard wood. Floor-to-ceiling inlaid bookshelves bordered a large meeting space separate from the foyer lounge, remarkable not for their dense, richly bound books, but the clean, bright sockets where the books should have been. A few design catalogs lay haphazardly about.

It was a proscenium without actors, a dream of style with the expectation of substance yet to come. A brass bell and tiny clapper hinged to an old telegraph switch sat like a mousetrap on the reception desk, a single whimsical and anachronistic detail in which some unfathomable amount of personal importance had been placed. It produced a feeble tinkle when I tapped it.

Through a second set of glass doors, a woman I assumed was the missing receptionist emerged at the summons of the bell. She looked like a sort of Barney's-meets-Betty-Crocker doll, clothed in an expensive looking retro skirt and matching camel-colored jacket. Her goose neck swept upwards to a vertically shellacked black cone of hair. Her smile was less welcoming than it was eerily permafrosted on her cheeks as if a severe side effect of the hidden contraptions which kept the hair under control. Her eyes were widened to the point of hypertensive detonation.

"Are *yooou* the Nick Bray we've been waiting for?"

"Have there been others?" Her neck pigeon cocked left and right. "Yes," I said, "I'm Nick."

"Hi, Nick!" she beamed. "Mackie Wallace, Chief of Staff for LaBar Partners Limited." I shook her hand.

I had not heard of a Chief of Staff outside of the U.S. Presidential office, but this was, as I came to find out, the nature of titles within the firm. Hyperbole with a straight face was the law of the land. It surprised me somewhat that P.J. LaBar settled for the title of CEO. If proportionally scaled to the other pollyanna titles in the office, he should have been dubbed *Grand Universal Global Thought Leader & Overlord of Marketplace Dynamics*. No one in the firm was hired full time with a title less than Vice President.

I heard the muffled sound of someone's apoplectic shouting within the bowels of the office.

"Mr. LaBar is regrettably delayed on a client conference call. May I get you anything while you wait?"

"Water, if it's easy."

I waited for the Chief of Staff to fetch me a water.

Was it prophetic that the second employee of LaBar Partners Limited I met was Shelby the Orangutan? After waiting nearly an hour for P.J. LaBar to wrap up his conference call, Mackie Wallace invited me deeper into the office. Walking down the long hallway, we passed a number of small, dark and empty offices with new computers waiting obediently for their masters.

At a turn in the hallway, I looked in on a truly cavernous corner office with floor-to-ceiling windows and a glass wall separating it from the hall. Running along the top of the glass hung a motorized movie curtain in the retracted position. Not only was the office equipped with a titanic, mahogany executive desk and an array of flat-screen LCD televisions broadcasting live feeds from a dozen news and financial networks, but it also contained a queen sized bench loaded with overstuffed pillows. Even more alarming was the super-sized commode partially obscured by rice-paper panels.

Distracted by the peculiarity of the decor, I nearly missed the sight of a full grown male orangutan siting behind the heavy desk, his lips parted in to reveal a goofy, white-toothed grin between his fatty cheek pads. He was enormously obese in that comfortable mammal way and covered in a copperish coat of fur. He appeared to be wearing some form of leather suspenders, but whatever they were holding up was obscured by his desk.

"And that's our Shelby," Mackie Wallace cooed, as though every modern office kept an adult orangutan. A Shelby in every ergonomic pot. Shelby waved ecstatically. She waved back at Shelby.

Deeper in, I met Chet Wallace, VP of Client Strategy, and husband of LaBar Partners Limited's Chief of Staff. I heard later that Mackie had joined the firm long before Chet, and had in fact been around for the firm's murky origins. Prior to his vice presidency at LaBar Partners Limited, Chet Wallace taught typing at what must have been the last high school in the U.S. to teach typing. He existed in a constant state of pants-shitting anxiety over client meetings, and it seemed his sole qualification for business was a healthy looking, midwestern, beef-fed athleticism that clients mistook for competency. Most of Chet's emails, remarks in meetings, and company-wide memos ended in multiple question marks. He wrote in the mode of perpetual surprise, and mixed Prilosec in his coffee grinder every morning.

The only less verbally articulate person in the office appeared to be LaBar Partners Limited's Vice President of Visual Communications & Brand Aesthetics, Ono Anna, who possessed a dubious MBA from Wharton with a concentration in PowerPoint design. She was a debilitatingly gorgeous woman, representative of the wildest and most improbable mixed-race dice toss of the millennia. To watch her walk through an airport was to marvel at the swath of male erectile calamity and feminine loathing she left in her wake. Mackie simmered incessantly with the suspicion that Ono was out to poach Chet. Ono's 600 word vocabulary emphasized affection only for her miniature Chihuahua and approximately 300 luxury brands of clothing, cosmetics, shoes, and handbags. She was exceptional at prepositions and eyebrow arching.

Turning a third corner, the floor changed from industrial carpet to a lush crimson pile illuminated by recessed halogen spots in the ceiling. We climbed a gradually rising spiral ramp. A variety of modern nature photographs hung along the carpeted walls. Each showcased giraffes in the wild, details of giraffes, moody Serengeti shadows of moonlit giraffes. At the top of the ramp, Mackie paused before two towering black doors. She reached into recessed panel in the dark and pressed a button. The winking red eye of a surveillance camera looked down on us from above.

"Yes?" a male voice spoke from hidden speakers. I could have sworn there was a subtle trace of reverb applied, Godlike, to the voice.

"Nick Bray is here."

"Excellent. Thank you."

At this point, Mackie trotted back down the ramp and left me standing in the near dark before the cyclops camera and the black doors. A number of metallic bolts sounded in rapid succession, and the black doors opened inwardly, powered by the steady whir of a hidden motor. Sunlight flooded the dark hall and temporarily blinded me.

When my eyes adjusted enough to ensure I wouldn't trip through the threshold, I took in a preposterously large penthouse office with a panoramic view of the green canopies and choked arteries surrounding Midtown Atlanta. In the center of the room on a raised dais stood a sacrificial-looking desk emblazoned with the firm's giraffe logos. A phalanx of flat screens covered the single non-glass wall. They displayed the offices and hallways I had just walked through, as well as a few muted 24-hour celebrity news channels.

"Nick, I am positively thrilled you are here."

It took me a moment to realize that my problem locating the voice stemmed from the fact that I could not quite see Pontius J. LaBar from his elevated position on the desk dais. He stepped out from behind the majestic desk of brushed aluminum. He was not quite dwarfish, but his height-to-girth ratio approached one-to-one. He wore a plaid Burberry suit with pocket square in a flamboyant arrangement of atmospheric blues. Under tightly groomed brows sat octangular, rimless glasses. His eyes retreated under pink, reptilian lids, occasionally flaring as though through nervous tick or imitation interest in your opinion. His nose blossomed with a hint of porcine lift. All of this fit together in a compact and polished package. Despite his physical appearance, he projected a warm, paternal wavelength of gratitude for your presence which was infectious and put you at ease. I didn't know that this mysterious and potent charisma was held back in reserve for meetings in which he desperately wanted something.

He motioned for me to join him on the platform and take a seat across from him at the desk.

"I am so very sorry I was unable to attend his memorial service." The image of his frenetic Porsche crossed my mind.

"I understand. I'm sure my father would have rather you took care of business. He was proud of you, of your accomplishments."

"I wish I had the chance to see him before he passed."

"I thought I might see... the... your—" I had never learned the kid's name that showed up at the memorial. "Intern?"

"Oh, no, no. We keep the interns on the lower floors. He has graduated, though, so he's no longer with us."

It did not occur to me to ask who the interns worked with on the lower floors, nor what the word "keep" meant, exactly. It was the word "graduated" that turned out to be more significant.

"Your father—" he briefly removed his glasses, but did not clean them. "He lit the spark. Without him, none of this would exist." He tossed both hands heavenward.

"Thank you. That might be overstating the case somewhat, though. But thank you for saying it."

"Yes, yes," he said. Difficult to know if he was reversing his position on my father's impact or simply moving along. "So, I understand you're a bit of a new media guru?"

I am still physically averse to those phrases. *New media. Web 2.0. The social web.* It gives me the feeling one gets walking barefoot through a shallow, still canal, the unseen mud, shit, and algae life oozing between the toes.

"I've been around it a long time, anyway."

"But you live in San Francisco," he insisted. "The cultural *heart* of it."

More canal mud. What I failed to understand in this first exchange with P.J. LaBar, was the notion that his questions, when he had already made up his mind about something, were merely mile markers for you to acknowledge as he confirmed the story he'd written for himself. True success within the firm depended upon not only identifying these disingenuous questions, but inventing ways to reassure and amplify his position. For example: the correct response to *So I understand you're a new media expert?* is not a modest and self-deprecating admission that it seems to be the kiddie pool you've reluctantly waded in for twelve years. Translated, what he had really said was, "I need you to pretend to be a new media expert for me, because there seems to be a shit-load of money in knowing the jargon, and no one here knows squat."

A good response on my part would have been an enthusiastic, "I should hope so, by now. I've been living and breathing it for 12 years." But the truly great response would have been a slightly arrogant and cool, "To be perfectly frank, I think the term 'new media' is an old media term. Through my experience, I've come to see it as the inevitable future of *all* media... and those who aren't with it won't be there to see it happen." Say this and his eyebrows would lift appreciatively as he memorized the phrase for future use in meetings. If I had said this, he would have responded, "And I couldn't agree *more*."

Why was this response his favorite sort? It would *shame* the clients. It made the clients feel stupid for having asked a troublesome, specific question. With the fear of appearing ignorant arose the consultant's most profitable environmental condition: The client's unwillingness to gamble their ego on due diligence. Thus the professional freedom to scatter fertile bullshit where green money grew.

"We have a number of very exciting client projects in the pipeline," he said. "Where I think you could enhance our capabilities is specifically in advising our clients on *all things digital*."

I braced for a question about resume. It never came.

"We would, of course, start you at the vice president's level. We would also like to establish a satellite office in San Francisco. It would be just you, at first, but as the office expanded, you would head it."

I imagined the orange profile of a giraffe stenciled on my bedroom door, Sagamore hiking his leg to cover the new paint smell.

"Do you have a few good suits?"

"I should probably get a new one."

"Not to worry. We have a fund to defray those expenses. I will make sure Mackie knows you'll need new attire. She will arrange fittings for you in San Francisco."

He paused to consult his BlackBerry, brow dark, mouth slightly open.

"Now. You are certainly wondering about compensation." He withdrew a PJL monogrammed card from inside his jacket pocket and placed it in front of me on the desk. "I realize it is a bit modest, given your cost of living in San Francisco, but I think you'll find that our executive team is compensated in an array of non-cash benefits."

If you added up everything I had earned in my adult life, it would have added up to a number less than the six digits on the card.

"It's a start," he said, enjoying the shockwaves of the knowledge that the number was beyond my wildest earning capacity. "Any questions?"

Aside from not knowing what my job was really, what was expected of me, or what sort of work the firm even produced (the headquarters bore no trace), I couldn't think of a single productive question. I wasn't about to ask why an orangutan had the second largest office on the executive floor. Definitely not what his suspenders supported. But I wanted to know about the giraffes. His face brightened and relaxed into a well-rehearsed speech.

"Oh! Yes, yes. The giraffe, as you say, or *Giraffa camelopardalis*, is a symbol of the firm's unique, even exotic, talents." He pointed at the image of the animal on the desk. "As you can see, *being the tallest living animal, it possesses a graceful neck to see the future and four long legs to stride ahead*." He paused dramatically.

The phone bubbled a light, Swedish sounding melody. He looked at the caller ID. "Ah. This is Randi Bevelecazzo in our New York office. Perfect timing."

"Hi Rand," he said. "I'm sitting here with Nick Bray, the promising young digital guru I told you about from San Francisco. I'm about to have Mackie send out a memo. He'll be joining the firm."

A woman's voice: "Fantastic, Nick. Welcome."

"Thanks." I had not, technically, accepted anything. But the zeros on that card made it abundantly clear where I was heading.

Randi continued, "As you've probably intuited, we're in desperate need of someone with cross-channel capacities. Someone who can interpret these innovating digital modalities for our Web 1.0 clients."

"I couldn't agree *more*," P.J. said.

Randi Bevelecazzo never said anything remotely straightforward, and if I had to put a percentage on it, I would say I understood less than twenty percent of her sentences. Clients lived in absolute terror of her opening her mouth.

"P.J., reach out to me later when you've closed with Nick. Welcome aboard, Nick."

I spent the afternoon mostly by myself in an office filling out paperwork sealing the deal. From time to time I heard dictatorial shouting from the penthouse office, but I could not make out the words. Mackie Wallace ran to and fro in her heels. No one else spoke to me for the rest of the day. I saw P.J. LaBar once more as he stood at the glass of Shelby the Orangutan's office, waving goodbye to the fearsome animal with his bulbous chin pouch. When it was clear everyone was packing up to go home around 5:45, roughly fifteen minutes after P.J. scurried from the office to catch a flight to his next client meeting, I gathered up my copies of the paperwork and left. Out of curiosity, I rode the elevator to the second floor of LaBar Partners Limited.

The elevator doors opened onto an unfinished floor, wiring and bare ducts suspended over a bare concrete floor. The fine white dust of concrete sawing coated everything. I did not explore the other floors.

An obvious group of rough-ridden prostitutes chewed gum in the tarnished brass lobby of the Grand Atlantan. That night I lay in bed thinking about my flight back to San Francisco. Some vague comments had been made about my travel arrangements for a client meeting the following week.

I wasn't interviewed, I was acquired. Nothing I could say would deter P.J. LaBar from hiring me. The morning I picked up the phone and dialed the number inside his invitation, I confirmed his suspicions. He had correctly identified in me the defining pre-qualification for joining the executive team at LaBar Partners Limited: Extraordinary moral lassitude.

In the morning, the car service swept me up from The Grand Atlantan. We idled in Atlanta's SUV-thick arteries for an hour. Still, I arrived early for AirTran's direct flight back to San Francisco. At check-in, I was informed of my business class upgrade.

In security, a glass display case presented all of the items which had been confiscated from passengers' carry-on luggage in the past year. Chainsaws, emergency flares, a sword, a weed whacker, boxes of ammunition, and a live grenade rested on black velvet. At the gate, I watched a man in flip-flops, a cowboy hat, corduroy shorts, and a white Sean John track jacket with gold piping unwrap his burrito supreme, nestle a quarter-pound pretzel dog inside, and surgically re-wrap the burrito.

Atlanta Hartsfield-Jackson International Airport. The crossroads of America.

Chapter Four

Nick's Crash Course in the Customs of the Country and a Surprise Visit from a Spiritual Advisor

In the months following my first trip to LaBar Partners Limited, I spent more time in airports than I did the luxury apartment the firm had rented as my office. The two-bedroom museum apartment perched on a corner of the 39th floor of The Tantamount Building just south of Market street in downtown San Francisco. (Tantamount to what, was not clear, but one intuited from the impeccable doormen and seasonally redecorated lobby, that it must have been tantamount to your own fantasy of exclusive living.)

Short of speech coaching, a hired army remade my life in the two weeks back from Atlanta's maiden voyage. A FedEx overnight box arrived with letter-press business cards, the newest model BlackBerry, and a black AMEX card in my name for expenses. A dapper, tactful man named Juno Flores at Nieman Marcus fitted me for three $3,400 suits—two conservatively pinstriped board room cuts and one edgy Danish costume in vaguely metallic fabric. I'm sure he was as mystified as I was as to why someone would spend over ten thousand dollars to put someone like me in suits, but he treated me in accordance with the money.

A color consultant from Thomas Pink coordinated shirt designs, ties, pocket squares, cufflinks, and tutored me in the peculiar origami of tie knots. The first call on the newly activated BlackBerry came from the interior decorator at Room & Board, who wanted me to make a decision about the leather color of the reproduction Eames' lounge chairs on order for the Tantamount apartment. Whereas my primary personal dilemma over seating up to this point was wet versus dry, dog hair versus mystery crust, I would now select the particular slice of the color spectrum which would grace my ass.

P.J. LaBar requested we purchase a "geographically appropriate iconic object" for each office. My first purchase on the black AMEX was a $7,000 "superfixie" version of the *Kidrobot x Nemesis Project* bike that Petey's Mission District irony shop sold, its white Aerospoke front wheel and rear powder-coated Miche Track hub welded eternally still. The decorators hung it with ultra-fine titanium thread from the living room ceiling under the requisite halogen spots.

P.J. created these extravagant havens at the firm's expense, largely under the pretense that it allowed members of the firm to have comfortable working spaces when we travelled to metro areas for the *street-level cultural research and trend spotting expeditions* we professed to be engaged in around the clock. The "New York Office" was, in fact, a an equally opulent version of the Tantamount on the Upper West Side, dedicated entirely to executive usage. When P.J. traveled to these cities, though, he didn't stay in the quiet ivory towers of the satellite offices. I suspect he chose the Four Seasons and Ritz-Carlton not solely for the service staff, but so that he would not be alone and unimportant in a city. His closest confidant, after all, was not eligible for travel, owing to the no-fly rule regarding five hundred pound orangutans.

On the roof deck of the Tantamount, Sadie and I split a bottle of 2005 DuMol Viogner, sent to me by Randi Bevelecazzo on behalf of the

New York office. The wind watered our eyes and kept the DuMol cold all the way through. A chaste but devastating tension simmered between myself and Sadie. I was uncomfortable with our age difference, primarily because I didn't know her true age. She had admitted to 19 after her initial 22, but I wasn't sure. Who would lie to say 19? Only someone younger. We watched the white hot river of commuter traffic snaking to the Bay Bridge. Light condensed into violet. We stood quietly on the edge of the barrier around the deck. She leaned her head against my shoulder. The entire undulating body of San Francisco lay beneath us.

"Not bad, Nick."

We touched glasses.

"To my mortgaged soul."

Sadie swallowed her whole last glass as if tossing back a shot of well tequila.

"This is definitely the *second* building I would fly a plane into."

"The second? How do you plan on surviving the first?"

"I mean my second choice."

"What's your first?"

"*Duh*. TransAmerica."

We walked across the deck to look at the TransAmerica building. It would always the TransAmerica building.

She squeezed my hand, and winked. Then she lifted her free hand and swept it through the skyline. She made a little jet noise.

"Not that I would." She dropped my hand. "Been done."

I asked her to live in the Tantamount apartment. I was only around it brief spells. As far as I knew, she had been drifting between friends' couches. She accepted.

"Strictly insurance," I said. "Just in case the TransAmerica goes down and you start getting the itch."

"Nice way to crown the moment, Nick."

"Just saying. I don't think you'll shit where you sleep."

She rolled her eyes. "Talk to your clients with that mouth?"

"Same one."

I was satisfied with the thought of her enjoying the apartment while I traveled.

Though P.J. preached a church/state distinction between home and work (a sermon that escaped him in practice as well, as it turned out), I didn't see much of a need to keep living in the athlete's foot and dog urine inspired atmosphere of the pigsty house on Hayes. I said my goodbyes to the frightful bony head of Sagamore and turned my old room over rent-free to Jake Hawkins, a poet and TSA passenger screener I had met at San Francisco International during my frequent trips through the gate of his metal detector.

Just like that I went from the half-a-burrito-a-day diet to patron of the literary arts.

I saw Jake at the airport more often than I saw him in the city. Though the firm boasted a healthy cash flow from equity positions in a number of unspecified but successful past clients, it didn't take too many leathery Eames chair reproductions and AMEX purchases extrapolated across the business to understand the enormous burn rate on LaBar Partners Limited.

In order to keep filling the funnel with money, Pontius J. LaBar had to pitch anyone who had even hinted at needing a "strategic partner." It didn't matter what our qualifications were. It didn't matter who the client was. P.J. LaBar claimed that we always had *extensive experience* in the industry in question.

I met Jake Hawkins at the beginning of a horrendous multi-city tour of new business meetings. Between trips, I had a lot of time to enjoy aspects of the city I had long since renounced due to financial hardship. This included walking to City Lights Bookstore in North Beach and browsing the poetry section. The firm supported almost any purchase I could conceivably link back to a billable client account, and so a couple of footloose days eating meatball sandwiches at Mario's Bohemian Cigar Shop and taking all-staff conference calls about PowerPoint slide transitions was the reward for long hours in ridiculous meetings in alien cities over lost causes.

I had taken to reading poetry on my business trips. It was short enough that you could read it between flight attendant and seat-mate distractions. You were supposed to read the same pieces through multiple times. It was written by people who theoretically cared about language. It also fit conveniently in laptop bags and seat-back pockets, and kept me out of SkyMall Magazine, whose advertisements only served to amplify the absurdity of travel.

It was in City Lights that I picked up Jacob Jude Hawkins' 2007 *Yale Younger Poets Series* prize-winning collection, *On the Tarmac*. Imagine my surprise when Jake Hawkins' face from the author's photo was sitting on opposite side of the security checkpoint at San Francisco International Airport. I stood stocking footed in the same state of disassembly as the other travelers, plucking laptops and gallon bagged toiletries, clutching my paper boarding pass, when I looked up to see Jake Hawkins' hair, like an explosion of enormous black palm leaves, cresting the x-ray machine.

His head was tilted down in the identical attitude as his contemplative author photo, which I now realized was a look of concentration. He was staring into the irradiated guts of each passenger's carry-on bag, divining which objects were safe and which ones were capable in playing a small part in the destruction of an airliner. Could his author photo have been taken on the job? It was the same moon face and thick-lensed, black-framed pair of glasses. The same medium length black beard. The man ahead of me set off the metal detector and the line stopped.

"Excuse me—are you Jacob Hawkins?"

"I am," he said without turning his head from the x-ray monitor.

"I have your book—the new one—in my bag." He adjusted his glasses up the bridge of his nose and waited.

The man holding up the line dropped his watch in a bucket, tried to pass through the metal detector again, and failed.

"It's a good book. I just... I mean, obviously you know that, it's a Yale winner, but... I don't mean this the wrong way, but what are you doing here?"

"I work. You are aware it is a book of *poetry?*" His voice, sonorous. Stripped of metal at last, the man holding up the line moved ahead. They waved me through. My body passed through Jake Hawkins' gateway to the limbo of boarding.

A headmistress' voice rained down from the girders: *"Attention! This is an important announcement from the Department of Homeland Security. The nation's current threat level is at ORANGE."*

And so it went:

In Dallas we met with a petroleum executive who wanted "to back a horse in this slow food game."

In Cleveland we landed a naming project for a pharmaceutical company. The lacquered, lasered, and enameled project manager we met with wanted a new name for a drug used in foreign state interrogations. Though banned for use in U.S. Military interrogations, it had to "sound American" to create the impression that it was the drug of choice among U.S. interrogators.

Naming projects were massive margin projects for LaBar Partners Limited. P.J. described a "rigorous, linguistic analysis process" in which we "study ancient roots, branches of languages, and the memes and phonemes relevant to the project" and then "map prospective names against the sonic blue ocean in the marketspace." Directly after that meeting, we convened in a Starbucks and dashed off a few invented names on the back of a boarding pass. We came up with Telluzol, Revealator, and Confestra. Randi would sit on these four weeks and then we'd present them on a conference call. Even if they rejected them all, we'd take $75,000 in the kill fee and retain the rights to resell the names next time around.

In St. Louis we sat down over beer cheese soup with a four-man business development team from a national beverage manufacturer and distributor who wanted to develop a new line of "terroir" bottled water. The story went that the water was collected from local taps which best represented the unique character of the communities from which it was sourced. Lamenting their limited exploratory budget of $2.6 million, they wanted to see if we would consider an assignment choosing the hottest markets from which this "local water" could originate, develop shelf-talker tasting notes, and conduct focus groups in six major cities.

It was hard to concentrate in the meeting, as the impish pricing analyst who was the most vocal advocate for the project kept rolling the Rs in terroir and pronouncing the last R. The silent, brick-necked executive to his right visibly flinched each time the Rs rolled, but did not say a single word until the meeting approached 5PM. The closer we got to 5PM, the more anxious he seemed to get.

P.J. LaBar, with $2.6 million dancing in his eyes, could simply not shut the fuck up over his praise for the idea. "The Nuanced Taste of America," he framed in the air with his hands. He was doing half of the "work" out loud as the beer cheese soup cooled to the hardened consistency it was already forming in our arteries. The executive, who's face had gradually wrinkled from a light grimace to the full-blown crumple of a mid-bowel movement grunt eventually cut P.J. off:

"All right, then. All sounds fine, fine. But one thing for sure: I want this on the YouTubes. You do all you're talking about *and* get it on the YouTubes." He looked at his watch and smacked his palms on the table. "Let's call this a day."

In Nashville at the Gaylord Opryland Hotel, a sort of waning Death Star for American country music nostalgia, a pair of tasseled and rhinestoned brothers pitched us on providing "a market segmentation study" for *Done Did It!*, a personal productivity system aimed at the country boy entrepreneur. Pontius always smelled the money behind bad taste. They were somewhere near the top of an inheritance food chain connected to a major tobacco products producer. The series, to be sold as a 6-disc DVD set, would include endorsements fromNAS-CAR drivers, mid-list country western singers, and an as-of-yet-to-be-determined line-up from Comedy Central's stable of gentleman red-neck comedians.

That night, I couldn't sleep, so I rode the Opryland shuttle bus to downtown Nashville and walked the strip of bars, BBQ, and music joints. A Hank Williams impersonator crooned at the tourists under the skinny neon signs. I had a 9AM flight to Newark for a new business meeting, but I couldn't remember the client. I was bloated and bleary, soaking up beer and trying to remember when the Opryland shuttle made its last run back across the river, when my BlackBerry's LED eye turned red, signaling a new email message.

A word here about Research In Motion's little terror maker: The LED light at the top corner of the BlackBerry was the device's most insidious design decision. It was literally a beacon for your mood. You prayed for green, always green, a placid lack of new information. At 6AM, when the Atlanta Office was well underway in their eastern time zone, my eyes would scan the nightstand for the winking light. When it was red by 6AM, my stomach churned with the knowledge of what awaited me; last-minute travel, ranting email messages, an urgent proposal.

To: LaBar Partners Limited Executive Group
<execs@labarpartnerslimited.com>

From: Pontius J. LaBar <pjlabar@labarpartnerslimited.com>
Subject: Canard!

I AM SEETHING! Canard has made fools of us ONCE AGAIN!

Tomorrow's meeting in New Jersey is OFF. HOW COULD THIS HAPPEN? WHY AM I FORCED TO WORK WITH SUCH AMATEURS? Regroup in home offices tomorrow morning to immediately begin a comprehensive battle plan for major client meetings ahead. They are at our heels at every turn. I do not think I need to tell you all how vital it is we move at the speed of the market... dead weight will be left behind!!!

Onward NOW!
PJL

P.J. lived in a festering state of envy over everything Canard Consulting did. When Canard launched their new website, P.J. saw it as the absolute pinnacle of design and functionality. Never mind that it was impossible to use and seemed to operate in a special fourth dimension of consulting jargon. He hated that their impenetrable air of exclusivity far surpassed his own manufactured enigma. His feelings of inadequacy were so deep seated when it came to Canard that any small defeat at their invisible hand would send him into isolation, seeking only Shelby the Orangutan's consolation. Tonight, he was undoubtedly in his room, ordering a rack of comfort ribs for dessert. He would be alone, mulling over how the ungrateful firm failed to understand the great sacrifices that were required of a chief executive.

Even Randi Bevelecazzo kept her distance when the Canard effect kicked in. She made it a point to receive a full massage at every stop of a multi-city tour. She may have been moonlighting as a hotel spa travel guide. She was certainly as glad as I was glad not to be returning to the Atlanta Office. After raining white hot Hell on the staff there, Pontius would disappear for a week or more, precisely at the time when his feedback would be required on all of the final proposals due to the prospective clients we'd just met with.

He would resurface first as a disembodied, staccato blast of bitter and injurious email missives, all of which would ignore the dozens of requests for him to review proposals and client work. This would evolve into an "all staff" call berating everyone for their gross incompetencies. The call would end with him slamming the phone down. When he would get around to finally opening the documents and PowerPoint presentations he was supposed to bless, a second wave of molten criticism would erupt. Good news would need to come to break the spell, or at least the forced diplomacy required of a client meeting.

A second email followed from Mackie Wallace with my revised flight itinerary.

No one knew anyone that worked for Canard Consulting. No one knew who headed up their brand management division. No one had ever accidentally ended up in a first class seat next to someone with the little winged logo of Canard emblazoned on a TUMI laptop bag. Randi Bevelecazzo claimed that someone in Manhattan had told her that Canard owned their own jet fleet with private pilots. We all more or less lived in fear that Canard would open an office in Tokyo or Paris, and that news would reach Pontius while we were traveling with him.

I was quite drunk by the time I made it back to the Opryland Death Star. I wandered the labyrinth of hallways, all of which seemed to lead back out to the roaring white noise of the glass-domed arboretum. A regional real estate trade show had kicked off that evening, and the theme park bars were heavy with white wine spritzered self-help platitudes and high hair. I found my way back to the room with the aid of a cryptic carpet coloring system, explained to me by an off-duty bellhop who was eager to pick-up a boozed real estate agent.

I called the Tantamount apartment, hoping to hear Sadie's voice, only to hear my own voice on the machine. I watched re-runs of *Antiques Road Show*. An old woman from Madison, Wisconsin brought a jewelry collection she inherited from her grandfather, and a man from Boston stood by to tell her (and the rest of the world) if it was worth anything. They knew the small marks that signaled authenticity. They knew what would rat out a fraud. She tried to look unmoved when he told her the brooch was a cheap Chinese copy sold at carnivals in the turn of the century. Now, when she imagined the moments through the decades when it had changed hands, she could hear the far-off laugh of a carny on the midway and catch the foul scent of farm exhibits. Three generations made a fool.

It was three A.M. by the time I finished up drinking the booze in the minibar. I dreamt of an army of appraisers descending on my father's memorial service, picking through the Don Quixote figurines. They conferred in small groups, working out the value of everything he had left behind. Gradually they worked their way to where I sat in his old wheelchair. They circled around and leaned in close to me for a final conference. Close, then closer, and I could feel their whiskers like my own father's on my face when I was a boy.

The wake-up call came at 6AM. In the shower, I thought again how we had not scattered my father's ashes after the cremation. They shipped him from the crematorium priority mail. What was left of him was in a sealed bag inside a cardboard box on the top shelf of a closet in Florida. He was next to the archive of cancelled checks and retired dictionaries.

Pontius and Randi were nowhere to be seen in the morning, and may have left the night before for all I knew. I was grateful for the black back seat of the car service limo. Grateful to be flying back to San Francisco and not further away to New Jersey.

My driver had a full Mark Twain mustache and looked prematurely old, as though he'd begun dying his hair black in his mid-30s and had stuck with the drugstore brand for twenty years. He asked me what I did for a living. I thought briefly how well Brooklyn "terroir tap water" would sell in San Francisco and felt my raw stomach burn. The driver's interest in conversation was always inversely proportional to my desire to chat. I was so at a loss to explain LaBar Partners Limited to the small-talking drivers and desk clerks, that I got in the habit of making up simple, tangible careers.

"I work in sales for a company that manufactures armored personnel carriers for the military."

"Oh? That so?" He looked up in the rearview mirror as though I deserved real attention.

"Yep. That's so," I said. My hangover sat like a block of melting cheese in my skull. The scenery blurred by in ash and green.

"Haven't met too many folks in my car connected with the military. APCs, huh. I hope you make 'em good," he said, leaning a little forward to merge with the morning traffic. "I got a son riding around in one right now."

The reflectors thumped under the tires. Would that I had noticed the American flag and yellow ribbon hanging from his rearview mirror, the kid in dress blues taped to the dash.

"This new line," I said, "it's practically impenetrable. Best yet."

"I hope ya'll send 'em over there soon. I hear that's just the thing they been missing." Our limo accelerated rapidly into the far left lane. A silent exchange of hand signals passed between my driver and a weaving panel truck.

"I don't suppose you got a buddy or two over there?"

I shook my head no. I knew when to stop digging, so I put down my shovel. I could see the steep profile of a jet out of BNA. The ride would be over soon. The driver glanced again at me in the rearview mirror. He knew the score.

"Mind if I smoke?" He didn't wait for my response. He rooted around and shook a cigarette from a pack in his chauffeur's coat. He punched the lighter in the center console and then cracked the driver's side window two inches.

"Don't worry," he shouted over the torrential wind. "I'll blow *my* smoke out the window."

A hop to Charlotte then a straight shot to SFO. I was sweating BBQ sauce in seat 1A. The flight attendant brought me a warm towel—sweet angel of mercy—and I carefully tracked the effect cabin pressure and altitude changes had on my bowels.

My seat mate, a leathery, reconstructed woman wearing a white tennis visor, paged through a glossy titled *Gun & Golf Quarterly*. She dog eared a page now and again and leaned towards the window, owing in large part to my smelling like a pork-savory ash tray. I attempted to read Jake Hawkins' book again, but couldn't make it all the way through the first poem, *Ode to Baggage Handler*. When the in-flight movie started, the window shades were lowered on the attendant's announcement, and we were all treated to merciful twilight.

The FAA's gift to me was preventing wireless access to anything. A gaggle of lobbyists somewhere were adding up lost hours of productivity at the behest of CEOs who suffered network withdrawal at altitude. Very few, it turned out, were writing postcards to their children. Word had it, VirginAmerica was going to fuck this up first. A day was coming when they would revoke this wireless prohibition, but for the upper underlings like myself, cross-country flight time was a welcome respite from the BlackBerry's jeweled eye.

I woke over the midwest, and by the look my seat mate gave me, I had been silently peppering the first class cabin with last night's transubstantiated Nashville cuisine. On the little ceiling television, two monstrous robots engaged in a form of mortal combat that strongly resembled scenes from a *Purv* video.

The captain in captain's voice interrupted the climax:

"Gooduhhmorning, folks… this is Captain Chuck Ferguson up here in the flight deck with first officerrrruh Ryan Andrews. Cruising along right now at 32,000 feet. Clear skies, good visibility. Air traffic control tells us pilots are reporting a light to moderate chop up ahead, so we'll be turning the seatbelt sign on here in… rrrrRRRroh, about 15 minutes or so. If you need to stretch your legs, or maybe make use of the facilities, now would be a good time to do just that."

My seat mate looked pointedly in my direction. I wondered if I had somehow succeeded in corrupting the flight deck as well, prompting the announcement. I fumbled with my seatbelt and stood uneasily, cutting off someone from coach who was making a mad dash for the forward laboratories. Suck it, coach. The galley was empty and haunted with blue-white light.

I opened the door to discover my father sitting on the toilet.

I slammed the door.

When I was thirteen, I fell backwards skateboarding and snapped my left harm in half. Literally, when I looked over to take stock of the funny feeling in my arm, it was bent in half, midway between my elbow and my wrist. I had shattered both the ulna and the radius, and muscle spasms curled my arm up like a cobra mid-strike. Before the pain confirmed this, though, I thought what I saw was a trick of dust and tears, that the light had been distorted to create this illusion of a freshly installed second elbow.

I felt precisely this way, standing in the galley of the 767. This image was not possible. I had opened the door on some careless passenger who'd left the door unlocked. I was tired. Hungover. Still, the image was clear in my mind.

The door edged open under its own power, the indicator above the door knob very much green and not the red word OCCUPIED. The flight attendants gathered empty cups and garbage from the rear of the plane forward. Before long they'd see me loitering by the flight deck door and shame me back to my seat.

I leaned to peer through the margin of the cracked door.

"Son, step into my office."

His overgrown eyebrows waggled above his gold-rimmed glasses. With his slacks crumpled on the floor, his leg stubs, as round as erasers, kicked freely in a mock dance. He was in one of his Fall semester teaching outfits, a v-neck navy cardigan over short-sleeved Oxford shirt and canary tie. I glanced away and back again, then pushed the door all the way open.

"A little drafty, don't you think?"

I stepped inside and locked the door. The fluorescent light did not turn on, so I stood in the overcast safety lighting, back flush against the wall.

"Didn't see this one coming, did you? Well, I have a message for you, son." He fluttered his hands in the air like a bed sheet ghost. "I was murdered! Avenge my death!" He fluttered his stumps.

"I'm kidding. I kid. Hamlet? Hello? Is this thing on?"

"You're not here. I am having a BBQ-hangover-induced hallucination."

"Is that the bouquet we're all enjoying?"

"You're dead."

"Indulge your old man. I know the secrets of the universe and you've got something better to do?"

"Why are you here?"

"What am I, the ghost of Christmas future? I'm your father, for fucks' sake. I'm checking in on you. You're the reality television of the afterlife and there's nothing else on. What else am I supposed to do?"

"Did you check in on mom?"

"Please. Thirty plus years, I think she's due a break."

"Fair enough."

"So here I am. Fire away."

"No legs waiting for you in the afterlife?"

"Maybe I earn them back. I don't know yet. Next question."

"Heaven? Hell?"

"Ah. It's a little more complicated than that. You know when you were a kid, and you had that ant farm in your room? You used to watch that thing for hours. Couldn't get you to sit still for a Cubs game, but ants! Sure, why not, hours of fun here, dad."

"What about the ant farm?"

"So it's a good news bad news thing depending on how you feel. The ant? That's you. The inside of the ant farm? That's what youperceive. What does the ant know about French film, new pussy, the continent of India, about Sinatra, about beef lo mien? Nothing."

The plane began a subtle bounce.

"What does that mean? That doesn't make any sense."

"Maybe take it this way: Don't sweat the small stuff. The big picture is bigger than you can handle."

"This is the wisdom of the afterlife? Chicken soup from your stumpy soul?"

"How the hell should I know? I just got here. Get back with me in a hundred thousand millennia. But, son, all the ant does is dig a tunnel and move the food around. That's it. That's what I want you to take away from this visitation."

The plane was bucking pretty good now, and I had to hold onto the sink to steady myself. The return to seat light bing-bonged red. A shuddering, knocking vibration racked the jet. My father hiked up his slacks over the stumps and kicked the hollow, cuffed sleeves around in his trademark vaudeville way of dealing with the whole no feet thing.

"One more thing," he shouted. The plane made some exotic metal fatigue noises, the Boeing Disaster Orchestra tuning up. "I can tell you why the Denver Airport is so goddamned far away from everything!

The gateway to the afterlife is under the Denver International Airport! I shit you not, a million souls in baggage claim!"

Someone smacked the door of the lavatory and hollered at me. My father grinned and punched the FLUSH icon on the toilet. The floor dropped. I bonked my head on the smoke detector. The ghost of my father swooshed into the blue cascade of the chemical toilet and was gone. I pitched forward and grabbed the plastic seat, heaving a technicolor arc of smokey abstractions into the empty bowl. Abruptly, the plane banked, and I was thrown backwards. The door broke open and I rolled ass-over-tea kettle into the galley.

Then, calm. As quickly as it had wracked us, the turbulence passed. I sat in a cold puddle of Spicy Bloody Mary Mix dribbling from the trolly. A flight attendant helped me up from the floor and ripped paper towels from the dispenser. Through the now open windows of the first class cabin, we were invaded by gold light and those fade-to-orbit blue skies. Everyone perched in their seats like yearbook photos and stared at me, the pale passenger swaying in the galley.

Chapter Five

Nick Enjoys a Fleeting Spell of Refuge Behind the Golden Gate Before Embarking on Serious Biz

Praise Indian Summer in San Francisco. Praise bare bodies in Dolores Park, praise the marijuana truffle man winding through the crowd. Praise the bums debating bum politics on the overlook up on 21st. Praise guys cruising on the high lip where the J-Church snakes up the hill. Praise the sweet and stubby haired lesbians in their army green culottes and white wife-beater Ts, slouching about unselfconsciously with crescent moon potbellies peeking through. Praise a city of dogs, an army of dogs. Praise a field of brown bagged beers planted in the hands of skeletal, sunburnt douchebags, the long lines into the concrete bunker bathrooms, and praise the holy Mexican guys ping-a-linging brass belled ice cream carts up and down the sidewalk.

Being in San Francisco again was like being amongst a crowd divinely pardoned back into the Garden of Eden. It wouldn't be for long, true, but it was good to be here. The temperature would hit a freakish eighty today, the wind barely a breath. The onshore flow had been reversed, the fog would sulk in the Pacific. Tonight the whole city would be on the streets, in the parks, sitting around shipwreck fires on Ocean

Beach.

Sadie Parrish stretched out on the unrolled rug we'd bought from the Salvation Army store on the way over. Her red hair flared around her head like the ecstatic Virgin Mary halos in gangbanger cholo tattoos. Her eyes were closed and the freckles on her chest were nearly luminescent. We weren't sleeping together. We weren't anything together. Being with her after travel was like passing from cold tunnel into sunlight; she sent healing shockwaves from her body in every direction. I was afraid of ruining it. I was superstitious.

I watched as she absent-mindedly stroked her bare stomach and talked about detonator assemblies using the common parts of keyless entry systems for cars.

"That's what they used to do for the roadside IEDs before the military started carrying signal jammers. The electronics come in from Iran, they build the bomb and plant it, and the spotters wait for the convoy to roll by." She raised her arm and thumbed an imaginary fob: *Bleep-bleep*.

"I may need to hard wire a secondary," she continued dreamily. "I thought an old iPod would be good for that. Lead wire from the power source in the iPod runs to the bomb jacket, a second pair of decoy headphones stuck in my ears. What looks more natural than a girl skipping through her iPod?"

Sadie had a colorful clutch of banking tattoos arranged in an AK-47 rifle shape on the calf of her left leg. Bank of America, Chase, Wells Fargo, Goldman Sachs, HSBC and a few so generic I didn't recognize them. On her right calf, the colorful logos of Chevron, Shell Oil, Mobil, Texaco, and a smattering of other petroleum companies formed the body of a tank.

"What do you think about the stomach?" she asked.

"I like the stomach," I said. She cracked an eye open at me and smiled.

"*Niiiick*. I mean what logos should I have done on my stomach. I was thinking Walmart and Starbucks."

"What about fast food logos? Since it's your stomach?"

"Mmmm. Not bad. I can see why they pay you the big bucks. Then I could put Starbucks and Walmart on my shoulder blades."

Now and then I found the talk of her suicide bombing depressing. First, I wasn't sure I believed her. But then when I did believe her, it wasn't just that I'd miss her, but that talking about the tattoos and the explosives and the triggers and the strategy felt like defensive small talk.

"Does it really matter where the tattoos go?"

"I don't know, does it matter to Jake where the words go in his poems? For him, sure. But does it matter in terms of what they'll find when they clean me up? Maybe on my feet, maybe the back of my head. I read in a DeLillo book about *organic shrapnel*. It's when bits of me actually become like fragments from the bomb, traveling at supersonic speeds, and like, I don't know, a year later, there you are having your cornflakes, and some little part of me works its way out of your skin and drops on the breakfast table."

She was sitting up on her elbows, staring at me from behind her knock-off Ray Bans.

"So does it matter, really, where they go? Will they put me back together again and say, 'Wow, see how cleverly she grouped these tattoos? There's a message here for us!' No. But it matters to me."

A homeless man in a wheelchair back-pedaled through the crosswalk with his one good foot.

"Does your brother ever visit you?" I asked her.

"*What* are you talking about?"

"His... I don't know. His ghost? Do you ever see him?"

I hadn't told anyone about my father's apparition in the United Airlines lavatory. I called my mother to see how she was doing, but I only heard her halting greeting on the answering machine, using that self-conscious tone parents get when they are alone, talking to bewildering machines.

"I had a dream about him once," Sadie said, sitting up now, her elbows on her knees, the elastic in her bra ragged and slack.

"Just one dream?"

"Yeah. No, I mean, I have dreams where he's in them, but I only had one where it was really him. Really, really vividly him."

"What did he say?"

"It was so stupid. He was excited. Like, Christmas morning eight years old excited. He gave me a big hug and kept saying, 'Sadie, it's gonna be so awesome, it's gonna be so awesome.'"

"What was…? Did he mean, your… mission?"

"No, no," she waved her hand around and looked at the ground between her bare feet. "I asked him, 'Tony, what's going to be so awesome?', and he said, 'When I get home, I'm gonna get my Camaro back. It's gonna be so *fucking awesome*.'"

She wiped her nose and laughed. "It was sweet, I guess. I couldn't remember ever seeing him so happy. About… an old muscle car. He spent every free hour restoring this 1968 Camaro in high school. So I guess that was the Camaro he was talking about. He totaled it about a week after he graduated. Drunk. Celebrating. Walked away from it, but the car was thrashed. He was depressed for the whole summer."

"Where was home, anyway?"

"Gosh, then? Just outside of Denver. Kind of out towards the airport."

"Do your mom and dad still live there?"

She lay back down in the grass and stretched.

"That's enough of that," she said.

That night, I received a voicemail from Randi Bevelecazzo. Pontius needed "the executive team assembled posthaste for intensive work sessions" on a new client. My flight information would follow. I called Randi the next morning, which was a Sunday, but since I was told to fly out Monday, I couldn't put it off.

"It's imperative we land a new flagship client, and P.J. thinks this is the next big one."

"Sure, great, I understand. But I just got back. We can't do this by WebEx or phone or something?"

"He says no. Atlanta isn't my preferred workspace, either, but what can you say? From a revenue perspective, there are no other optimal pathways."

"Who's the client?"

"It's a need to know secret. He also wants to plan the company retreat."

"What retreat?"

"See you at the Atlantan Terrace, Nick. Monday night."

Randi's husband was somehow connected to professional sports, though the exact nature of his purpose wasn't clear (an emergent theme in most of the firm's personal relationships). I suspected he was somehow involved in personal success coaching for the newly minted cretin millionaires, especially in the arena of reputation management and damage control. I thought of their marriage as a "mobile marriage" in that most of it happened through text messages and cell phone calls, though periodically they would cross cities.

I was certain of one thing: Whatever he did outclassed our pay scales by many multiples, so Randi's work for LaBar Partners Limited was something of a hobby from an income perspective. She found pleasure in the manufactured urgency of consulting, and each client meeting was like a trip to the zoo for her. I could never shake the feeling that she explored our clients with an air of imperial superiority, sizing up the natives for clever cocktail party banter later. I was certain, somewhere back in time, she was in the corner of a drama club photo, wearing a little black beret, and next to her name it said *future director*.

I squandered Sunday in a funk, anticipating business meetings. Feeling punitive, I took Sadie and Jake out to dinner that night at *Boulevard*. Jake wasn't privy to Sadie's masterpiece-in-motion and shook his head over the patchwork logos exposed below v-neck and hem line. Our Luxor Cab departed in a rush for nowhere.

"You're marrying permanence to irony," Jake lamented from the curb, the little tracer of his joint tracing crazy eights. "It's a grave aesthetic offense, young one. The child of permanence and irony is obscenity."

"What permanence?" Sadie said. She grabbed at the joint, but Jake held it high above her head in a taunt.

"If the logos outlast the companies, it's not obscene," I said.

"God damn it, give it up." She jumped far short of his reach.

He laughed and lowered the joint slightly, only to jerk it away.

"Jump, my trout of America," he commanded.

Sadie crouched to jump, but lunged up and decked him in his round gut instead. He whooped over, coughing a cloud.

"Ha!" She snatched the joint from his hand. "The flesh is weak!"

Smoke vines writhed up Jake's kinked beard. He gathered air while Sadie held her smoke, face a knot.

"You're right," he said finally, and pointed at me with his thick index finger, the nail gritty from picking out seeds. "If the logos outlast the companies, it's not obscenity. It's nostalgia."

"See," I said. "There's hope for the future right there." Sadie passed me the joint.

"No, no, no," Jake shook his head. "Nostalgia is the greater offense."

We occupied the valet space in a little human triangle. I handed the joint back to Jake and he pinched it. A charcoal Maserati flashed its high beams at us. Sadie bound up her copper hair before clearing the space, her blue dress electrified by the xenon headlights. Jake removed his glasses and turned them between his thumb and forefinger on his t-shirt. The Maserati claimed the socket of the white curb.

"I feel under dressed," Jake said. "It looks a little black tie in there. Do we have a quorum for a steady diet of Mission pinball and whiskey instead?"

The valet held the door for the driver of the Maserati. The driver eyed Sadie's inked calves. I wondered if he appreciated her calves, or recognized his employer's brand.

"No, absolutely not," I said. "Black AMEX trumps black tie."

"And so the wise consultant consults," Jake said.

"What are we in the mood for?" Sadie asked.

"Everything," I said. "We want everything."

Jake was working security in the morning, so I offered to have the car service swing by and pick him up on the way to the airport at 4:45 AM.

Any day Jake worked the security queue at SFO was a good day to fly. I believed there was no way Sadie would appear if Jake was among the huddled masses.

All the good Dolores Park did for my soul was rudely disassembled by the preparations and mechanics of air travel. I hated flying so early, but I hated arriving in cities at night more. I dragged my carry-on behind me like a still-tethered afterbirth. I could already hear the flatscreen televisions on the other side of security firing hot tracers of CNN, MSNBC, and FOX News.

The smell of old carpet and watery coffee and industrial disinfectants traveled in crosscurrents. I heard others' conversation adorned with the names of a variety of humiliating, competitive reality shows.

Jake emerged from a break room or staging room on the other side of security and took his post at the silvery x-ray machine. His quasi-cop uniform of white shirt with embroidered names, ID badges, American flag pins and stitched-on, gold-shield patch made him look like a security clown for a Ginsberg reading. He adjusted his glasses and took up his post in the x-ray monitor's glow.

An elderly woman shouted into her cell phone as we snaked through the small, plodding serpentine line.

"I'LL BE ARRIVING AT THREE!" she shouted into the brick shaped phone, evidently to someone chasing tornados on an active runway in Hell. "NO, THREE! OKAY, DEAR. OH! OH! DID YOU REMEMBER TO FEED GOLIATH HIS PILLS? NO, THE BLUE PILLS! DON'T FORGET OR HE'LL MESS THE CARPET SOMETHING FIERCE DEAR."

Was Goliath the dog? Was Goliath the cat? Was Goliath the husband, cranked up in his hospital bed in the living room?

Sadie and I played a game in the park. We picked people from the crowd and imagined what they would look like when they got old. She projected the subtle slump of a shoulder into the octogenarian's humped osteoporosis. I predicted how far the chins would recede, the overbite yellow, the eyelids fall. Spot the Italian girl with the licorice hair who would give up on the dye in her sixties, letting the silver roots blossom.

Who would have the liver spots among the tattoos gone blue?

"Not me," Sadie would say and wink.

All the thoughts unasked. *Did you own horses? Who were your friends? What role did you perform in your high school play? Do you look like your mom or your dad? Did your hamster die when you were six? Who was your first kiss, your first fuck? What did your room look like? Did you lie on your brother's blue sleeping bag and stare up at Colorado star fields? Did you pretend to be a cowboy, or did you favor the Indian side?*

Some you could guess at. But all of these questions of her past were off limits. She spent late nights on Internet message boards. There were sympathetic vets arguing the classification of their cranial injuries with VA paper pushers. They posted trophy kill photos from garbage choked streets. They embraced screaming metal music with titles like *Petitioning the Empty Sky*.

Fresh disappointment and betrayal minted daily. There were no jobs. They could no longer be relied upon, it seemed. They were now machines too fierce to be trusted in the delicate civilian orchid garden. People knew people who had access to resources she needed. She had youth and beauty. This was her currency.

Sadie was wealthy with it. She stepped from the bathroom in a loose white towel and the sight of her alone might shred you with desire.

As I prepared to pass through the checkpoint at SFO, Jake gave me a copy of *The Voice at 3AM and Other Poems* by Charles Simic.

"This, brave traveler, is as far as I can escort you," he said, visibly suffering from his third of a thousand dollars' worth of Boulevard's wine list.

"Be strong and daring now."

"Fuck you, too," I said.

He laughed through his black beard and his butcher block teeth shone white.

My BlackBerry winked its un-Visined cyclops eye. The hive buzzed in Atlanta.

An itinerary for planning sessions in Atlanta included a graduation ceremony for a LaBar Partners Limited Intern, an "intensive mission briefing" for our mysterious new flagship client, and a "pleasant announcement concerning our annual year-in-review retreat."

Pontius clearly felt the need to summon the royal court around him.

Waiting at the gate, I sketched out a few notes for a novelty deck of tarot cards for business travelers. Kinked paper airline pillow in halcyon blue, automatic hand dryer light, eternal no smoking sign.

Flight delay. FAA-mandated crew rest time.

I flipped randomly to a Simic poem titled *This Morning* and scanned the first stanza:

Enter without knocking, hard-working ant.
I'm just sitting here mulling over
What to do this dark, overcast day?

I remembered last night I had a dream. I was at my mother's kitchen table, like a white formica pill, and when I shook the box of Grape Nuts, my father's cremated ashes spilled into the bowl. We were out of milk. I picked up the spoon to tuck in. Because that's all we had to eat. And that was the ethic in my father's house.

Chapter Six

In which Canard's Insidiousness is Evident, Details Surrounding the Mystery Client are Revealed, & Shelby's Appetites are Discovered

Interns at LaBar Partners Limited were ranked using the "shirt color system" according to Chet Wallace. He told me this over a beer at a sports bar not far from the venereal Grand Atlantan Terrace, whose own bar had handsome brass taps which hadn't flowed since 1951. Randi Bevelecazzo and Pontius were engaged with "senior executive" meetings that night, a fact I was thankful for, and so Chet's anxious company was a good opportunity to learn a little more about the perverse inner mechanics of the Atlanta Headquarters. Mackie Wallace called three times during our conversation to make sure he hadn't lied about his whereabouts.

The shirt color system was divided in three: Chocolate shirts for new interns, robin's egg blue for mid-level interns, and a bright salmon for the top of the food chain. From here, all of the Interns (should they make it that far up the ladder), would graduate to "Associate" status.

"But there are no associates in the firm," I said. "It's all VPs or SVPs."

Chet Wallace raised his eyebrows.

"They either quit or graduate," he said. He stared into his beer, shoulders hunched forward.

"Do you mean graduate from college and move away?"

Chet set his teeth in a no-lip grimace.

"You'll see tomorrow."

"And what's with the lower floors of the firm, anyway? I stopped the elevator on one during my first trip here, and it wasn't even built out."

"Sometimes the interns stay on that floor."

"Stay *where?* It's concrete and duct work and wires."

"On the floor. There are bedrolls."

I laughed. "Seriously, Chet, I have a hard time imagining college students—unpaid college students at that—subjecting themselves to foam bedrolls on a bare concrete floor."

He leaned further forward.

"They're not college students," he whispered. "They're drop-outs. Transients. Runaways. Craigslist posts. He gets some of them from Greyhound and Amtrak stations."

Chet dropped me back by the hotel. Outside of the Atlantan Terrace, a heavy-set black man in enormous sunglasses argued with the valet of the Atlantan Terrace about leaving his mother-of-pearl Escalade (24" chrome rims) running in the semi-circle driveway while he ran in to "*check up on sum thangs*" with his girls. Either from morbid stupidity or an extreme death wish, the valet held fast to hotel policy. A stoic white kid with a white ball cap tilted sideways sat in the passenger seat, flicking his switchblade eyes around.

"Beans, nuggets," the kid muttered as I passed them like a ghost.

The room service zombies hunched over their carts in threadbare tuxes were more frightful than the bejeweled and waddling hookers haunting the corridors. All night I would hear the sunk costs of their sweaty labor through thin walls.

The nature of professional work was about the same for everyone, but the suits were different.

I called the Tantamount apartment in San Francisco and Sadie answered. I told her what Chet said about the interns. She endured my travel lament admirably, probably because she was resting comfortably rent-free in its profits. She told me she was going to take BART out to Concord to see a tailor about making her a jacket.

"You never struck me as much of a clothes hound," I said.

From the room next-door I heard a whip crack.

"You know I'm not," she said. "Ask me what I'm wearing right now."

"Are you going to get frisky now that I'm three thousand miles away?"

"What are you wearing, Sadie?" she asked herself in a mock-deep version of my voice. "Nothing but your apartment!" she answered herself and laughed and laughed.

"Normally, this would be an incredibly erotic conversation for me, but you have no idea what's going on in this hotel. It's completely infested with appalling whores."

"You mean like the one I'm on the phone with?"

"Ouch. Touché. But ouch. What's so special about this jacket, anyway?"

"Well," she sighed. "It's kind of a single use jacket," she said. "Wear once and destroy."

The bomb jacket, then. I didn't want to know more about that, not tonight. But I would not say "be careful." I would not, I would not.

"I should go. I'm getting up early, plus this east coast time thing kills me. I may not come directly back to San Francisco. I think they're going to fly me to this mystery client meeting directly from Atlanta."

Not many days begin with complimentary biscuits and gravy and end with rape. But then again, not many people are privy to the inner workings of a global brand capital management consultancy.

We assembled in the conference room promptly at 8AM, as instructed. Mackie Wallace, Chief of Staff, pushed in a food cart of steaming biscuits and hot sausage, a small chef's hat Pontius required her to wear for these duties pinned in place. P.J. LaBar arrived fashionably late for his own meeting and spent most of an hour staring into his BlackBerry, munching from a private bag of powdered donut holes he had picked up on the way into the office.

Ono Anna pushed her biscuits around with a spoon and Chet Wallace studied her breasts while she did so, much to his later peril, when the Chief of Staff would have him at home alone. A Brown Shirt Intern cleared our dishes, and I noticed that he did, in fact, look as though he had recently shaved off a thick beard, owing to the tan line on his cheeks and the fish-belly color of his jawline. Randi Bevelecazzo showed up around 9:30 looking well massaged. By 9:45, a Blue Shirt Intern nervously fumbled with the expensive LCD projector, trying to connect it to Ono Anna's laptop. The projector didn't work. Fifteen minutes later, we were underway (the power cord had been unplugged).

On the first slide of the first presentation of the day, P.J. stood up from his chair and charged the wall.

"What is THIS!" he jabbed at the projected slide, which contained the LaBar Partners Limited giraffe next to a line of text which read: "Special Fall Planning Session."

"Can someone tell me why *this font* is next to *our logo?*"

By all accounts, it looked like the standard sans-serif cool kid font that we used in all of our presentations. Ono Anna withdrew a pair of reading glasses from her little gold Fendi clutch purse and studied the slide.

"That is our font," she said.

Pontius' nostrils flared. Chet Wallace's sweat seeped through his shirt.

"Ah, yes, but the clumsy KERNING! Am I the only one who sees that the devil is in the details? That Canard has taken two million worth of business from us this month alone, and that the root of that failure lies *RIGHT HERE IN FRONT OF US?* Fix it!"

Ono Anna dragged her laptop to adjust the kerning and knocked over her chai tea. A dainty shriek peeled from Pontius. Ono dodged to the side, preserving her Jimmy Choo heels, and the Brown Shirt Intern, lacking paper towels, lay his body down on the table to soak up the hot chai with his Thomas Pink shirt. The chai had to be scalding hot. He grunted deep in the back of his throat as he slid from side to side mopping up the spill.

"That's the kind of outside the box thinking we expect," Randi said from the corner of the room. "Emergency solutions."

Pontius bolted from the conference room to gather his nerves. It would be up to Mackie Wallace to coax him out of his office so we could start again.

We'd been in the conference room over two hours and not a single bit of work had been done.

Though he was in his penthouse office above us, via email (red flagged), Pontius notified us that we would begin our meetings after the Brown Shirt Intern had been honored with a ceremony celebrating his promotion to the Blue Shirt Intern class. Ono Anna was ordered to prepare the standard intern promotion PowerPoint, which involved dropping in a few "action shots" of the intern during his time at LaBar Partners Limited. Given that he'd been in the office less than a week, Ono Anna shot a few digital stills of him standing against the front doors of the office in his chai-wet shirt, and a staged shot of an empty tea cup turned on its side on the conference room table.

She asked Chet Wallace if he would help "light the shot." He was eager to assist. As was the Atlanta Office tradition, the intern could choose a song to be played during his "shirting ceremony." He chose AC/DC's "Hell's Bells." Ono dropped the pictures into the presentation, downloaded the song, and we gathered again in the conference room.

Mackie Wallace drew the blinds and dimmed the lights. AC/DC thundered through the conference room at apocalyptic volume levels. The presentation began, a lengthy cycle of LaBar Partners Limited stock shots from over the years, filled with substantially thinner versions of Pontius with his mouth half open, dispensing million dollar advice. The slides proceeded with star wipe transitions, followed up with the dropped in pictures of the scalded intern taken just an hour before. Since the presentation outstripped the song, the music had to loop, and AC/DC cranked up a second time with its solemn bells.

Randi Bevelecazzo took a call during the presentation, and I can only imagine what the receptionist of the next spa thought as she tried to confirm Randi's facial and body wrap reservation while AC/DC crackled in the background. Eventually the presentation ended. The last slide read: "Congratulations [INSERT INTERN NAME]!" Ono rapidly advanced the slide. Pontius was absorbed with his BlackBerry and missed the error.

The "shirting" itself was a humiliating affair in which the brown shirt intern stood in the front of the room before the executive team while Mackie Wallace undressed the intern from the waist up and then clothed him in the new shirt. Standing in the white hot light of the projector, it was clear he had second degree burns across his chest and belly. The only blue shirt available in the office closet was too small for the intern. He flinched and grimaced as Mackie tugged the buttons together. When it was over, the thoroughly tormented intern stood like a scarecrow fit to burst while we golf clapped.

We broke for lunch.

This was not the graduation Chet Wallace had warned me about. That would come later in the day.

Looking back over what's been written about my time with LaBar Partners Limited, I see I may have given the impression that my entire job consisted of flying around and attending ridiculous meetings. This is inaccurate. While it was a solid sixty percent of my time, an additional twenty percent was allocated to conference calls and emails leading up to and following up after the meetings. Since LaBar Partners Limited never produced any hands-on, tangible work ("execution" was the trivial afterthought behind "strategic and tactical planning"), my minimal computer talents accompanied me as a vestigial tail might.

So what did I do for the remaining twenty percent? I wrote proposals.

Like a high-paid Vegas trick, it turned out I was good at simulating what my Johns wanted. I excelled at dirty writing. I had a passable knack for mimicking the tone and jargon that Randi and Pontius used in their lengthy (and seldom read) proposals. I could speculate. I could manufacture unfounded predictions based on shoddily supported data. Expert opinions with emphasis on the opinion. Both as formal as an invitation to a feast for foreign dignitaries and as impenetrable as a dissertation in bullshitology, the art of the "LaBarian" proposal resided in a delicate seasoning of solicitousness, arrogance, and glancing allusions to the impossible ad hoc promises that squeezed from Pontius' cheeks during face-to-face meetings.

They were the architects of half-truths. I was the draftsman.

With the intern wrapped in his expensive cotton agony, the kerning in the fonts repaired, and a second wave of food consumed, we were free to begin the meetings. Again. Inexplicably, the priority item on Pontius' agenda was announcing his plans for the costly retreat, not the mystery client.

With Pontius in the role of Pat Sajack and Randi Bevelecazzo playing Vanna White, next year's retreat was unveiled to us one amenity at a time. We were destined for the Ritz-Carlton at Reginald's Plantation, a few hours outside of Atlanta. Those of us flown in would be treated to first class flights. Our spouses and partners were invited.

We would be chauffeured from the Midtown offices to the lavishly manicured wilderness of the Reginald's Plantation. It featured trails, a vast and pristine lake, horses, a world-class spa. And from 8AM until 9PM every day of the four day weekend, we would be in meetings. Each of us would be expected to orchestrate a presentation on our area of expertise. All meals would be eaten together. The event would culminate in a small awards ceremony, recognizing each executive member of the firm for their contributions over the previous year.

In short, we would be gathered within view, but not reach of, a luxury resort.

I wondered if Sadie would consider a new soft target for her mission. If the company lasted that long. The truth of the matter was, LaBar Partners Limited was going to go broke if it didn't land at least one, possibly two large clients. This was not explicitly stated by Pontius to the members of the firm, but it was in the air. Randi Bevelecazzo had told me as much, and in the Atlanta Office conversations stopped abruptly when one turned a corner. The low voices and wild eyes told the story of a plane in flames with too few parachutes aboard.

And they rightfully should have feared the ship going down. The only marketable skill one took away from a consultancy was maintaining the facade of marketable intelligence. The whole lot of us were utterly unemployable due to a lack of skills or motivation, or a combination of the two. Furthermore, the time inside LaBar Partners Limited was the professional equivalent of saying you had spent a year or so within the alternate universe of a black hole.

After lunch, we had a half hour to check email and gather ourselves for the final two items on the day's agenda—the briefing on our next client meeting and the graduation ceremony. I stood for a few minutes at Shelby's glass office and watched him watch FOX News. He clapped from time to time and curled his lips.

An announcement over the office intercom broke my reverie.

"Vice President Nick Bray, please proceed immediately to P.J. LaBar's office."

It was Mackie Wallace's voice, and I could see her making the announcement from the receptionist's desk.

"Mackie, I'm right here," I said. The Chief of Staff scurried from her post.

I was unsure, but it seemed as if Shelby was pleasuring himself to the image of the talking head on FOX News.

I found Pontius in his penthouse chamber, surveying the view and eating an enormous Chick-fil-A sandwich he had assembled out of the parts of three other sandwiches. His desk was littered with wrappers and waffle fries, like the strategy board of a colossal WWII battle. The waffle fry Allies were in dire straits. The great white light of an Atlanta noon glinted off the bun butter on his chin.

I noticed that he had a new Porsche somehow parked in his office. Not a model—an actual showroom-fresh Carrera 4S parked on the carpet. Later, Chet Wallace would tell me he had a replica of his "driving Porsche" helicoptered into the penthouse office so he could look at it while he worked. This was his "watching Porsche."

He spoke with his mouth full, and not directly at me, but as if I was a figment of his imagination he was addressing.

"Wheehabbamoll," he said gravely.

He lowered the sandwich to his belly like a pair of field binoculars.

"I'm sorry?" I asked.

Pontius chewed and swallowed and rested the sandwich on his desk. There was an air with Pontius that he was always in a stage production of his life, so that no interaction with him seemed natural. Of course he had an audience—it was the crowd of self-created critics and demons which he carried with him everywhere he went. I wondered—was it a father, an ex, a mother, or a successful brother he competed against?

No, it was always Pontius before the judgement of Pontius, every day. As he bastardized and bent his identity into the forms that his paying masters preferred, how could he not help but lose some central self? Without stage, who was he? Once the sense of himself was split and shattered, would not a hundred other varieties of Pontius appear in his mind, ready to nitpick and examine every word? He was his own public, and in short, he was afraid.

He plucked a cold, salted waffle fry from his desk and nibbled the edge, as if testing the authenticity of a gold coin.

"Nick, we have a mole in the firm."

"A mole as in a spy?"

"Yes."

"*Canard is operating from within,*" he whispered.

"An intern, maybe?"

"No. Too easy. I am afraid the rot is at the very highest level. It pains me greatly to admit it. That it... *escaped* my eye for so long. But nothing else makes sense. It is the final logical conclusion. And with these high profile meetings ahead of us, we cannot afford to let the mole rack our lawn."

I did not believe for a moment that one of the executive team was a double agent for Canard Consulting. It was not a logical conclusion of any kind. I was afraid that some of Pontius' self-critical voices were now being cast in the role of his competitors and enemies. I also thought for a moment he meant me.

"Randi is already aware of the situation. We're making plans to rout the mole. But I wanted you to be on your guard. You must tell no one about this."

It was just never enough to have the drama of the client meetings, the travel, the preparation and micromanagement of the PowerPoint presentations, or the interminable client dinners. There always had to be manufactured drama from within. The ceremonies, the retreats, the big systems for a little batch of con artists.

"Who's the mole?"

Pontius picked up four fries from his desk in a stack and pushed them into his mouth. He chewed savagely and the mauled potato jumped in his mouth. He took a long pull from his jumbo sweet tea.

"It is Chet Wallace," he said quietly and belched.

"Well, if you know, why haven't you fired him?"

"Ah. The obvious move. No, no. We have to send a message," Pontius said, tilting his head towards the crumbs in his crotch. "Plus, I'm sure you agree, we need to know how much they know. Plans are in motion, I assure you. Just be careful what you say to him."

"Does Mackie know?"

Pontius shook his head. "No, I'm sure he's hidden it from her. Alas, it is certain their whole marriage is a sham. It is really something to behold... how long Canard has plotted this take down of the firm. I wonder if they were guests at the wedding. These Canard jackals spare no one."

I looked at the Porsche while Pontius reengaged his sandwich. Inside the ghost of my father pretended to drive. He was hunched over the steering wheel with a kid's snarl on his face, making engine noises as he drove.

"Now this is a wheelchair, son!" he shouted from inside the car.

Pontius made no sign he'd heard a thing at all.

I don't know why, on these trips to Atlanta, I didn't add a day on the end to fly down to Florida to check in on my mom and scatter my father's ashes. All I could think about when I was in Atlanta was flying back to San Francisco and hiding out as long as possible before the BlackBerry summoned me back to the crippled city. But I considered going home on this trip. It seemed we were charging down the hill, all 18-wheels white hot and smoking, the brakes burned out, and the runaway truck ramp was the only option. Who would miss me? What could they possibly say? Would they honestly fire me? Absolutely not.

But who was I kidding? I knew exactly why I wasn't leaving. I was becoming accustomed to the conspicuous consumption. I was weighing myself against the earthly riches and I found myself lacking. And there was Sadie, of course. I didn't want to find out that when the money well went dry that my companionable enemy of the state would find herself a new silent partner.

Meetings resumed.

"We're facing a game changing reality for the firm," Randi Bevelecazzo said. She tented her fingers under her nose and made a point of looking us each in the eye. "The potential revenue stream from this prospect is an order of magnitude larger than any other we've represented. Segmentation studies, messaging, voice work, naming projects—there's no end in sight. *And*—"

"International travel," Pontius LaBar filled in.

"Very exotic locations," she continued. "Beyond the map. Far off the grid."

Sweet Jesus. I could already see myself standing next to an Alpaca at a mountain base camp while Pontius screamed that his Alpaca was not equipped with senior-executive-level amenities.

"If we land this one, folks, we're talking expansion. Major expansion. Possibly a London office." Pontius was already spending the money yet to come.

"Until the client meets us each personally, we can't reveal the specifics of their business model," Randi said. "But I want you to spend time this week concentrating on these ideas: Exclusivity. Anonymity. Experience as destination. Mandatory leisure. Off-grid manifest fantasy."

Pontius nodded as though his neck muscles were keeping his heart pumping. "Yes, yes, yes," he said. "Well said. I couldn't agree *more*."

"This client was a long-time contractor for the U.S. Military," Randi said. "This project will be their first civilian enterprise. Keep this background in mind. We'll meet in Las Vegas next week for the formal presentation."

"Are we presenting, or are they presenting?" Chet asked.

"Both," Pontius said.

"What are we presenting?" Chet asked.

"Our capabilities," Randi said. "And our analysis of the industry."

"Our extensive past work for exclusive luxury travel clients," Pontius said, his eyes fixed on Chet's damp hairline.

"Which clients? What past work?"

"Details!" He smacked his fist on the conference table. "We'll need a deep dive on the current state of luxury travel to exotic locales," Pontius said. "Ono, make some notes: I'm envisioning jungles, mountain vistas, private jets."

"And visualizations," Randi said. "We'll want dynamic visualizations of luxury travel data. Bubble diagrams and tag clouds and global heat maps. It would be great if we could present a 3D fly-through of market realities. We must reveal ourselves as badge carrying authorities of the algorithmic age."

"Oh, yes, absolutely true," Pontius said. "Bravo."

Randi believed every presentation, whether or not there were sufficient data sources, required colorful moving charts which provided a more complicated and speciously informative view of the simple sentence that could sum up a point. The point of her animated graphics was not to elegantly reveal the connections between concepts or separate information from noise, but to encase a feeble-brained generality in a rotating, flashing, bewildering interface, and reinforce it with a saturation bombing of jargon. Clarity, thy name is Cambodia.

Most of this would fall on Chet's plate, and he knew it. Ono would spend four hours on Getty Images picking out stock photos. I would write a few obscure paragraphs about travel which would be spoken by Pontius over a new age soundtrack. Chet would navigate the minefield of the actual PowerPoint presentation. In twenty minutes, tops, he'd have explosive diarrhea from the anxiety.

"Before we break for much earned rest, I think we should take care of the day's graduation."

Chet cast a knowing look my way. Pontius clicked the intercom.

"Mackie, send in the intern."

Randi looked at her watch and stood up abruptly. "If you don't mind, I'll take a pass on this today. New business calls to make."

Pontius curtly bobbed his head. When Randi had left, he mashed a button under the table and the large black curtain covering the rear wall of the conference room retracted to reveal Shelby's cage. The two rooms were joined by a thick glass door with an intricate locking mechanism embedded in the floor and the ceiling. When the curtain reached it's full height, Shelby bounded around the room with great gusto, clapping his hands. He spun circles and rolled head over heel.

Pontius walked up to the glass door and rapped on it with his knuckles, making soft hooting noises into the glass.

"Get your harness," he coaxed. "Go on, Shel, get your harness!"

Shelby the Orangutan waddled to his desk and opened the deep bottom drawer. From inside, he withdrew the harness I had seen him wear on my first visit. Only now, with the unobscured perspective of the conference room, I could see the harness was attached to a sizable orange strap-on dildo.

Pontius had the harness fashioned out of vintage Hermes leather pieces and specially fitted for Shelby's purposes once the old orangutan's own equipment was wilted past its prime. Shelby secured his harness and clapped and waggled the orange phallus with pure joy, as though he'd been reacquainted with an old friend unexpectedly.

"Go on now, Shel, hide in your cave," Pontius cooed. Shelby mimicked Pontius and extended his pale, crooked index finger in front of his lips in a shushing motion and crawled under the space beneath the executive desk in his cage.

Pontius chuckled and dropped into his rocking conference room chair, arms folded over his chest.

Mackie's voice broke through the conference room intercom speaker.

"Should I send him in now?"

"God, I never get tired of this. Wait until you see the look on his face, Nick. Yes! Yes, send him in."

An intern I'd not met walked down the hallway, wearing the bright Salmon Shirt which marked his status at the top of Intern Mountain. He turned and entered Shelby's office through the now unlocked door to the hallway. The glass door whooshed shut on hydraulic hinges and automatically locked. At first, the intern did not notice us sitting in the conference room behind our own glass partition. He tugged at the cuffs of his shirt and looked around, evidently confused he was alone, and probably bewildered by the raw smell of fur, overripe fruit, and animal shit that was miraculously sealed inside Shelby's office.

When the intern did notice us, he cocked his head like confused dachshund and drifted towards our glass wall. Pontius made a dandy little *hello* wave with his fingers.

Just as the intern reached the glass door to the conference room, Shelby the Orangutan launched himself from under the desk, his orange dildo bobbing like a bright whale hook from his crimson crotch. Pontius howled when the intern twirled to face Shelby. The intern lost his footing in a slick of orangutan shit and slipped backwards, braining himself on the chrome door handle to our conference room. In a matter of seconds, Shelby was upon him.

Suffice it to say that Shelby was well-versed in the use of his bespoke harness.

Chapter Seven

An Evening for Nick Upon the Wheel in Sin City

Say what you will about the myth of the $2.99 steak-and-egg breakfast, the men buried in the flower gardens, and the beatings in Binion's parking garage, Las Vegas is not as much in love with the past as the people who come there. It is not Las Vegas that meditates on vintage glamour and Rat Pack swinger swagger, but the people who start telling stories when they board their flights in St. Louis, Ft. Lauderdale, Newark, Cleveland. They carry in their mouths the names of the old casinos like personal currency. From the insurance salesman in a sleepy downtown main street to the president of a long-haul trucking company in Chicago, they will tell you on approach how they remember when it was Bob Stupak's, how there was nothing further north on the Strip than so-and-so, how there was a fire, how there was a strike, it was all you could X-for-Y, how this one time, and then, and you shoulda seen the look on, and we were comped this suite, and the pit boss was breathing down our necks.

And what they see when they land, when they break out of the airport loop into the patchwork flaming desert turning ceaselessly with bulldozer and crane is not what is actually there, but the same thing they saw the first time they piled into the bowling alley scented Blue Bell Shuttle on a $1.00 transfer to the Golden Nugget in 19XX. Inside of them is still the same spooling turbine of anticipation, the one that began whirring in their chest when they studied their dog-eared copies of *The World's Best Blackjack Book* published in '81, and imagined themselves at that holy green semicircle where they would add up the faces and tick off the aces, subtract the low cards and divide by half (if you had to play the double deck—*hah!*—table).

Never mind the casinos had long installed the shuffle masters with fourteen decks, and you couldn't touch the cards anymore. Forget the fact that they razed the long pits of card games with condo-sized complexes of networked slot machines. They could tell you when poker rooms were in and washed back out again and rolled back in with high tide. All of this was apparent, it was staring these eager old players in the face, but in between their fingers they could still feel the dirty white clay of the Horseshoe's $2 chip between their fingers and the scrape of the newly opened deck lightly inviting another hit on the green felt.

Gambler's nostalgia. Stand, split, double. The Christmas morning joy living in the hearts of grown men.

As my father was, I was a member of this tribe.

But the city of Las Vegas was not. Las Vegas would level itself if it thought the rewards were bigger in the next incarnation. And it knew they would be. Las Vegas had no attachments, had no bias, had very little memory. Las Vegas romanced money and dynamite. Las Vegas had no passion for the turn of a single card. It measured time in the probability of a trillion deals and terawatts of electricity.

What I came to love Las Vegas for was not the slim possibility of jackpots, but the assured anonymity. Las Vegas tracked you through a million eyes, but you were nobody but your money. Las Vegas was absolution from the self.

We were on final into McCarran International. In any other city, I hate arriving at night, but in Las Vegas it is the only way to arrive. The pilots never fly through the great beam of the Luxor. Client meeting or no, I was always glad to arrive.

Hello land of no time. Hello, luminescent pain killer.

My father, despite his career as a tight-fisted literature professor, also had a small-stakes passion for gambling. When I was 21, he took me to Las Vegas for my birthday, a trip which had been long promised since the age of about nine. When I cleaned out his office, I found the tiny memo books where he recorded each session at the tables. BN $2BJ +17. (Binion's, two dollar blackjack, won seventeen dollars). GG $3CS -21 (Golden Gate, three dollar Caribbean stud poker, lost twenty-one dollars).

He set a loss limit for the trip and worked from there, recording his take or loss for the trip by session. After he lost his legs to diabetes, he came to appreciate the accessibility in Las Vegas. Sidewalks as wide as runways. Ramps for every stair, elevators, and low-rider blackjack tables with reserved seating. Toilet stalls as big as studio apartments. Shorty urinals. The accommodating ramps of a civilized desert.

I fully expected to see him on this trip for LaBar Partners Limited.

The flight attendants vocalized their gambling jokes over the P.A. *Ladies and gentlemen, welcome to fabulous Las Vegas, Nevada. The local time is 9:43 PM.* An appreciative woo from the East coast travelers, the gift of a reversed clock.

I waded through the cavernous baggage claim, a model American refugee camp. The cab driver took me for a fool and drove the long way around from the airport. It was a well-known cheat. It doubled up the fare on the meter. I didn't say anything until we reached theVenetian Hotel & Casino, and then asked him if the number on the windshield was for the Las Vegas Taxi Authority. I wanted to ask them a question about the fare.

He looked up in the rear view mirror at me and said, "Must be your lucky night. Free fare today." I stepped out of the cab twenty-five dollars ahead and left myself behind.

Who was this Nick Bray guy, anyway? Never heard of him.

I knew Pontius LaBar did not gamble. He hated Las Vegas, and would be entombed in his suite, ordering room service. Chet Wallace would be frantically assembling a PowerPoint presentation. Pontius had rightly assessed the risk of Ono Anna opening her mouth in the meeting and was left behind in Atlanta. And well, the Chief of Staff had to herd the interns. Randi Bevelecazzo? She was so booked with spa treatments that she'd only be out of her bathrobe long enough to attend the client meeting, whoever it was. It wasn't a casino, that was for certain. Casino owners were micromanagers, people with the hearts of small business owners who had arc welded their attention to detail to the mad man's vision of excess. Hustlers who had matured, but still recognized the other hustlers.

I called Sadie.

"Any chance you can hop a red eye to Las Vegas?"

"Sorry. I'm on my own no-fly list until the big day."

"You ever consider Las Vegas as the venue for your really big show?"

"Who would even notice?"

I did not ask her about her jacket. If she had it, I didn't want to know what she did to get it. I just hoped something didn't go wrong with it before she needed it. Explaining how the Tantamount apartment's Eames chairs were borne flaming into the Financial District would be tricky.

"Ooo! I got the American Airlines logo done yesterday. Did I tell you this already?"

"No, you didn't. Where?"

"It's my new tramp stamp."

"How poetic. Lower back pain."

"I thought you'd like that. Come home soon and see it."

There wasn't much more to say. When I was away from her, I felt how acutely she was not attached to me. We were seat mates with different final destinations, except she knew hers.

The LaBar team was scheduled to meet the next morning at 8AM in front of the casino, on the bridge that spanned the replica Venetian canal where the motorized gondoliers puttered through the resort. A car service chartered by the client would pick us all up and drive us to their offices. With everyone locked up for the night, I had Las Vegas to myself. Less than ten hours, but that was enough.

Sitting in the great marble mausoleum toilet closet of my suite, I paged through a glossy gambling magazine. Steve Wynn had proposed the construction of a new casino off the strip— a massive five-tower complex of windmill hotels, themed after the adventures of The Man of La Mancha himself, the venerable Don Q.

Dr. Michael W. Bray was out there somewhere tonight. I would try and find him. He wouldn't be on the Strip. I was certain it was too expensive for him, even in the afterlife.

He would be where it all began. He would be downtown.

In 1986, my father was thrown out of the Golden Nugget Casino for trying to look at the other players' cards in $5 Caribbean Stud Poker. The game isn't played much any more, but in its heyday, it was a real casino builder. The odds in favor of the house are notorious. Of his loss limit, my father specifically reserved a whopping $50 exclusively for a single session of Caribbean Stud.

Each player wagered five bucks to get a five card hand. The dealer then received a five card hand. Two of the dealer's cards were turned face up for the players to see. The remaining three were hidden. If you thought your hand was strong enough to beat the dealer's, you backed up your five dollar bet with a $10 bet. Your hand had to beat the dealer's hand.

But the real draw of the game was the bonus system. For each hand, you wagered an optional single silver dollar chip to make a run at the jackpot and qualify for the bonus. If you beat the dealer, *and* the dealer's hand qualified with an Ace-King or higher, you were paid a bonus for your hand. A pair of kings or better paid a small bonus, with progressively larger bonuses for trips, a straight, flush, and so on. The big daddy bonus was a royal flush, which paid out a gigantic jackpot prominently displayed on an ever-ascending money odometer above the table.

For Dr. Michael W. Bray, no single game in the entire casino represented as much thrill and heartbreak as Caribbean Stud Poker. The cards were machine shuffled and laid out face down for each player. You were not allowed to touch the cards until the dealer had received their hand and the remainder of the deck was spit out of the robot shuffler for the next deal. At that point, the dealer performed her benediction, flashed her hands to the eyes in the sky, and said *Good luck, everyone.*

What every Caribbean Stud player loved was the moment between the dealer's well wishing and the gradual squeezing out of the hand, one at a time. Because if you thought hard enough, if you respected the cards, focused all of your energy, summoned and sharpened all of your desire, the suits and values could change before they were revealed. The hearts would keep coming. The faces would multiply.

Once your hand was revealed to be a likely loser, most players were very casual about how they handled their cards. The players were not playing against each other, they were playing against the house. And since it was a single deck game, it was helpful from time to time to see that your neighbor might have one of the queens the dealer could beat you with. Or you could see that all of the 7s were out, so that straight wasn't coming. Because of this, looking at the other player's hands was strictly forbidden. Most dealers recognized that the advantage this gave the players was so minimal compared to the roaring money vacuum that the game represented, that they hardly bothered to enforce the no-look rule. But one pit boss was not so lax.

So in 1986, with his 10-stack of $5 chips withering under the casino's mathematical advantage, my father ignored five warnings to keep his eyes on his own hand. Security hoisted him to a back room, photographed him, and blacklisted him from the Golden Nugget for all eternity.

Well, not for eternity, of course. Just the span of mortality. And that's why I knew that I would find him haunting the Golden Nugget Casino.

The cab dropped me at The Plaza Hotel end of Fremont, and I passed the Golden Gate quietly expiring on the corner. Outside of the Nugget, people stared, zombie faced, up into the curved, white portico that covered Fremont street, waiting for the Fremont Street Experience light show to begin. The luminescence of the casino's eponymous signs washed the grey promenade in a shifting sherbet tide of shadows. The smaller places had become gift shops with lip balm, water, and novelty dice.

Fremont's cockroach of strip clubs squatted invincibly in the center of it all. They were all smearing towards complete obscurity, like lipstick degrading on a wine glass. Sinatra's "Luck Be a Lady" reverberated through the old canyon.

"A lady doesn't leave her escort.
It isn't fair. And it's not nice.
A lady doesn't wander all over the room
and blow on some other guy's dice."

The Golden Nugget casino was the last old broad at the Fremont Street garden party holding on to her dignity. Most of the others had surrendered long ago, understanding that the crusties that picked downtown were fixed on cheap food, nickel slots, and the option to put their cigarette out on the floor if they were so moved. The Nugget polished the glass and brass, swept the marble floors in the lobby and made sure the dealers felt like hosts and not armed guards. It did not reek of a hundred million cigarettes smoked in foolish hope.

He was there, of course. Standing at the very table where they had blackballed him some twenty plus years ago. The Caribbean Stud table was long gone, and despite being prime time, the table was empty and locked down, thousands of dollars in chips under the glass and steel cover. Slots doodled and warbled. Scattershot cries of victory and disappointment crashed from afar.

Then I realized he was *standing*, or at least his ghost was standing, the wheelchair gone, the stumps no more.

"Look who finally decided to show up," he said and studied his watchless wrist. "Stop off for Keno at Binion's coffee shop on the way down?

"They don't even do that any more. Do you really still need a watch in the afterlife?"

"Come on. It's a prop. Time is infinite. The beginning is the end. I look up my Omega, I see my Alpha. What is it with you and trying to get the drop on the secrets of the universe?"

I pointed at his legs.

"Looks like you earned your feet."

"Earned nothing. Turns out it's a location-based thing. Don't ask me. Some places I get 'em, some places I'm back to stumptown." A security guy as big as a refrigerator in a gold coat eyed me sitting at the empty table.

"I'm in a free fall, Dad. Isn't this about the time you dispense with some life saving wisdom? We're in Las Vegas, it's a sentimental location for both of us."

He drew a large rectangle in the air with two fingers (BIG) and pretended to toss cards through it (DEAL).

"Seriously, this is the moment.. This is where it happens. Three on, two outs, full count. What am I supposed to do now?"

"Don't put it to me like that. Death is the final release from parenting. Aimless suffering is your father now. Take it to heart and spread the word to the rest of the answers-in-the-back-of-the-math-book generation."

"Bullshit. I don't believe you. You wouldn't be here if that was the case. You spent your life teaching literature, humankind's search for meaning."

"So *you* say! I taught literature as a defense against the chaos of the universe. There's a difference between a defense against oblivion and meaning, son."

"Fine. Well, this has been illuminating, dad. You know, I have a meeting tomorrow morning. Feel free to drop by then and we'll see how this little existentialist conversation withstands a roaring turbine of consulting bullshit."

I stood up to leave.

"Don't go yet. Stick around and I'll tell you why men gamble. Walk with me. I might as well use these feet while I have them."

We strolled up the pit towards the blackjack tables. The dealers dragged their cards out of the white plastic shoes and flipped the cards. Chips moved, players clapped, players groaned. We watched a man split a pair of eights, hit an eight, split again, double down on each hand, hit three tens, and lose to a dealer's 19. The man crumpled and fingered the black chip he told himself he wouldn't break.

"Oh, that used to feel like hell," my father said.

"So, why do men gamble?"

"Here it is, Nicky. It's a universal barometer. It answers the question, 'Does God love me?' I win, God loves me. I lose, God doesn't.

It's a divine sign of preference."

"He must change His mind a lot. You're telling me there's a God?"

"I'm telling you why men gamble. It isn't the money. The money is the container for the answer. The bet is the question. How much money do you have on you?"

"About three hundred."

We stopped at an empty roulette table. The dealer broke off the thousand yard stare and smiled. Minimum play, $25 inside the line, five dollar chips.

"What do you say, son? Let's have some fun. Let's ask God some questions on your behalf."

I bought a hundred bucks in five dollar chips. The Gambling Ghost Dr. Michael W. Bray clapped once and rubbed his hands together. "All right, here we go son. Team Roulette. The bastards can't see me cheat now. You pick four spots, and I'll pick the fifth."

I cupped five chips in my fingers and dropped four of them on numbers.

"Put one on black twenty," he said. The wheel had begun to spin. The dealer whipped the white ball into its groove. I placed the $5 chip on black twenty.

"No more bets," the dealer said. She wiped her hand back and forth above the felt. The wheel slowed. Gravity drew the ball out of orbit. It skipped along the ridges and settled into the slot for black twenty.

"Black twenty," the dealer said. She placed the little lucite monolith on the chip to mark the win. She washed my four picks from the field and stacked up the 35:1 payout for the black twenty hit. $175.

"Looks like you're in good with God, son. Grace shines upon you. Now let's hurt 'em."

By 2:40AM, there were two security guards in gold jackets standing behind me, two on the opposite side of the roulette table directly across from me, and I could feel every camera in the casino twitching imperceptibly as my father told me the magic number and I placed my sure thing on the winning spot. I had over $24,000 dollars in chips on the table, and a second dealer had been posted to help with the payouts and coloring up the chips. I turned reds to greens to blacks to purples to pinks. As had the crowd now playing with me.

I didn't make a noise when I won, but even in my stunned silence, passersby began to take notice of the mounting chips and the demonic accuracy of the last chip I placed on the table. A woman from Omaha placed a chip on mine. A retired Army colonel picked up the trend. The noise started with them. Then one more. One more player. Soon, the table was overwhelmed. Why they didn't shut down the table was beyond me, but I suspect it came down to one guy at the head of casino security who knew I was cheating, but it was killing him that he couldn't spot it. My father had taken up a position across the roulette table, facing me from between two of the security guards.

"They love you, the universe loves you," my father said. "People know your name and you're leading them to easy money. The casino is taking a hundred thousand pictures of you a minute. You're going to be these people's big Vegas story for years. And yet you look like the koo-foo bird shit in your Cheerios. Have you figured out yet why you're so unhappy? Black twenty again, by the way."

I placed the bet. As I did, so did the table. Black twenty it was. The players roared. I looked up at my father, and he was not the wise-ass ghost of the afterlife. He was Dr. Michael W. Bray of the podium, of the chalk-throwing, lecturing variety. He was not smiling.

"You prefer losing," he said. "It's very comfortable to sit in the can't-win position for you. Red six."

I placed the bet.

"The universe is force feeding you good luck, and it's like torture for you."

Red six hit. Everybody got paid.

"Now what are you going to do with all that responsibility, son? Are you going to roll with it? It's choosing you. You've got that cosmic advantage. Now it's on you: What do you do with it?"

The dealer asked me for my bet. Some of the players had placed their own. A few were holding back chips to see where I would play. I stepped back from the table. A security guard touched the coiled wire at his ear.

"That's right," my father said. Then his voice a little louder: "That's right! Go on now, you know what comes next. You quit!" His cheeks were red, his face creased and full, as he was when I was younger. "You quit! Because that's what you do! You're a quitter! Go on and quit! YOU'RE A QUITTER!"

The security guard nodded at the dealer. The dealer spun the wheel, the ball spun inside. A security guard touched my shoulder. "Sir? How about you come with us now."

But I was looking at my father, climbing onto the roulette table, the bets undisturbed under his black shoes. He screamed at me: "QUITTER!"

"Keep it," I said to the security guard. "Keep it all. Just keep it."

"No more bets," the dealer murmured.

"QUITTER QUITTER QUITTER QUITTER!"

I heard the security guard tell the other security guard what I'd said. The apparition of my father quaked with rage on the roulette table, invisible to the players. I stepped back to see if they would let me. No one held me in place, no stiff grips on my arms. Perhaps somewhere the man behind the eye in the sky got the message and told security to let me go. I turned my back on the table and walked straight for the exit to Fremont Street. My father's screaming became high and indistinguishable from the moneyed mania of the casino. In a minute I was again in the back of a black cab racing towards the Strip. He may have had legs, but he wasn't running after me.

I was only out about a hundred bucks, which is what I knew would happen when I opened my wallet in the first place.

Chapter Eight

The Tale of the Client, the Mole, & the War Room

The California king-sized bed remained tightly wrapped. I watched the dawn bleach Vegas from the twenty-fifth floor suite. The mechanized blinds on all of the floor-to-ceiling windows were retracted by their invisible motors. High, concrete clouds muted the desert sunrise. Directionless white light rose in the room like flood water. The shower was dry and cold, the chocolates on the pillows unmoved. The apples and bananas in the crystal bowl on the living room table would pass unbitten and unpeeled from the bowl to the garbage untouched, as they would in a thousand rooms more or less like mine. My suit remained folded in the carry-on, as it had since Atlanta. My jeans and shirt smelled of downtown's cigarette ash. The angry, anxious, and indecipherable emails bridled behind the blinking red eye of my BlackBerry.

They're smart, the architects who built magnificent hotels but also understood that windows should never open all the way.

Yes, I could walk away. Leave the suit, leave the suitcase, leave the laptop. I would never talk to any of them again. Take what money I had accumulated and hole up until it reached zero. I would take the

Charles Simic book of poetry and forget the rest. I was an hour and a half by jet from San Francisco. How much longer would Sadie be around, anyway? Why was I doing this?

Instead, I compromised. It went like this: I emptied the fruit bowl and filled it with cold water from the shower. I placed it carefully on the marble sink counter. And without checking the voice mail, the email, the text messages, I plunged the BlackBerry into the cold water.

It put up a good fight. The red eye, distorted though it was from the bottom of the bowl, winked for most of a minute before winking no more. I held my breath while it died.

I would simply go into everything blind today. Because if I read one raging email from Pontius, listened to one rambling voice mail from Randi, or scrolled through an abbreviated and panicked field of text messages from Chet, I wouldn't make it to the meeting. I would taxi to the airport and disappear.

I took the BlackBerry from the water and shook it out. I tried to turn it on. It was retired from service. I let it dry out in the sink while I took a shower, knowing full well it wouldn't turn on, and it would be a few days before the firm ordered a replacement for me. Another small act of plausibly deniable defiance. Another small act of rage in a larger commitment to capitulation.

I dressed in my suit and tightened my tie. I hooked the dead BlackBerry to my belt. I looked liked a six hour layover in an airport chair after a red-eye flight.

Chet Wallace stood in the valet circle, his free hand fluttering in his slacks like a trapped bird, his other clutching his BlackBerry. Pontius and Randi were nowhere to be seen, which was par for the course. They were notoriously late for their own meetings, and I knew we'd be shooting the shit with the client's car service for at least fifteen minutes. It was a studied tardiness, to be sure. Probably a business tip Pontius read in a musty guide for salesmen published in the 1960s. *He who has the spare time to arrive early for his meeting is broadcasting the wrong message to the prospect. Arriving a few minutes late to a meeting increases a fellow's perceived value.* Chet noticed me when I was close enough to knock him over. On his screen was a miniature chihuahua in an old-fashioned bellhop's costume. His teeth were on edge.

"Where have you been? I've been trying to get a hold of you since last night."

"BlackBerry died."

"You forget your charger?"

"No, it's dead. Bricked. Gone to the BlackBerry hereafter."

Counter to the climate, which greedily sucked dry every living thing, Chet was sweating through his shirt at the belly. He holstered his BlackBerry and jammed his hand into the other pocket. His pants were whipping like pennants.

"We met for breakfast at seven to go over the presentation. P.J. hated it, of course. He had a fit. He's threatening not to come to the meeting. Randi is trying to talk him out of his room."

A line of taxis idled for the day's crush of primetime morning flights. The cabbies read newspapers in their cars, listened to A.M. radio. The forecast called for storms, doormen were bantering about flash floods. The sidewalks were empty of the stoic Mexicans who flicked the glossy call-girl cards at the passersby.

Chet groaned, and a fart ripped from his suit.

"Oh, God. My stomach is killing me," he said.

"Bad room service?"

"No. I haven't eaten in a day. It's the *stress*. It's not enough that P.J.'s pitching a fit about this presentation. Mackie's breathing down my neck." Chet grunted.

"What about?"

"She thinks I'm fooling around with Ono. Where the fuck is

P.J.?"

"And you're not?"

"What? No! Of course not."

Chet looked about as guilty as D.B. Cooper would have had he shown up at a bank with a sack full of cash to deposit and a parachute trailing behind him.

"I guess you just happen to keep photos of chihuahuas in costumes as your BlackBerry background?"

A calypso beat of firecrackers rocketed from Chet's pants. He bowed slightly at the waist and shut his eyes.

"God damn. It was supposed to be just the one time. That was the agreement. One time. But now she keeps sending me pictures of her fucking dog, and—in the costumes, I—okay, it was like three times. Maybe four. But I think she was asleep that one time, so does that count? Ugh, what am I going to do? I think P.J. might know. I think he may have told Mackie. I think I'm going to shit my pants. Christ, here comes Randi. Keep this to yourself, would you?"

Who was Chet kidding? If Pontius knew, Randi knew. I didn't say this to Chet in order to preserve our last shred of breathable atmosphere. Whatever Ono Anna was doing with Chet, it was more about destroying Mackie than enjoying Chet. I wondered if she had amatching bellhop costume for him. However radiant Ono might have been with her legs over your shoulders, it wasn't worth the price you'd ultimately pay. But then again, I was probably just hard-up and a little jealous.

The casino doors whooshed opened and Randi appeared by herself. Her face wrinkled perceptibly, catching Chet's draft. He looked away and rocked on his heels. She studied him, and I recalled my lunch meeting with Pontius in Atlanta. Perhaps there was more to Chet's intestinal distress.

"So. Are we doing this solo?" I asked Randi. She had picked up a latte on her way out to meet us.

"P.J. will be here," she said. "Where have you been? We really could have used your input for our collaborative breakfast session."

"Dead BlackBerry."

Two black humvees turned into the traffic circle.

"That's us," she said, lifting her to go cup in the direction of the humvees. I had expected limos.

They were not the humvees of the ghetto fabulous variety. They looked like the automotive horsemen of the apocalypse. Blacked out wheels, black windows. Red dust. Antennae arrays. I felt a little ill, as I had nightmares from time to time in which they came to take Sadie away in vehicles just like the ones that were here to escort us to our meeting.

Pontius joined us on the sidewalk just as the humvees arrived. He didn't say a word, just shot daggers all around from behind his tiny, stop-sign glasses.

The men who emerged from the humvees wore black cargo pants, black ball caps, bulky black vests and had prison-hard bodies. They were wired and sunglassed and inconspicuously armed. The man who held the door for Randi had a gothic necklace of letters which said *I BLEED JUST TO KNOW I'M ALIVE.*

We drove far from The Strip, far past the warehouses, and far away from the subdivisions huddled around golf courses. We left the interstate and set off down a cracked and weathered blue highway, rising into the low mountains. Pontius and Randi rode in the lead humvee and I sat in the back of the second with Chet. The driver rolled up the cracked window when we turned off the paved road and followed the lead humvee's plume of dust into the desert itself. We were on a road the men knew from habit and GPS, and from time to time clipped messages on their radios cut through the still, cool air inside the humvee.

After a time, we arrived at a concrete bunker checkpoint. The humvees slowed but did not stop. We climbed a short hill, and on the other side, a small compound unfolded in beiges, browns and tan. Squat, windowless buildings that looked as though they waited for an airstrike dotted the landscape. Further on, I could see a black, unmarked airstrip with a commuter jet inside a metal hanger. A helicopter waited under overcast skies.

We were deposited outside a building somewhat larger than the rest. The men in the humvees drove away, and we stood together silently in a lashing desert wind. A man emerged from the building wearing a business suit and oversized aviator glasses. He was in his fifties, still formidably muscled, with a tight perimeter of buzzed white hair around his bald crown. He extended his hand to Pontius.

"LaBar Partners Limited, call me Mr. Z. Let me be the first to formally welcome you to *Rendition Vacations*."

The main building was one entrance to an underground network of rooms and passages. After a thoroughly disorienting series of turns, ramps, steel doors and stairs, we gathered around a low-lit mahogany colored conference table in a high-ceilinged room. Darkened flat panel screens hung on the walls. Once seated, Mr. Z offered us water.

"Welcome to the War Room," Mr. Z began. "I don't know how much you all know about our business model. I've had a number of conversations with Mr. LaBar, but let me bring the rest of you up to speed on our operation."

"Yes, please do," Pontius said.

"For years, my team has specialized in serving the transportation needs of a number of government organizations and agencies I'm sure you're all familiar with. I don't think I need to enumerate their acronyms here. Suffice it to say, business has been very good the past seven years. But to be blunt, the gravy boat is running thin on gravy. A certain spotlight has been turned on our activities which has in turn decreased demand somewhat. Fortunately, about a year ago, we started to look for ways to take our skill set to the free market, civilian population."

Mr. Z withdrew a slim controller from his jacket pocket and pointed it at a large screen. A slideshow of foreign landscapes began to fade in and out. Tropical jungles, high snow-dusted mountain sides, vast gold and red deserts. These were not stock photos.

"Stunning," Pontius said.

"Yes," Mr. Z said. "Stunning is the word. You can bet people are stunned when they see them for the first time. And for all intents and purposes, these places don't exist. Some say 'off the map' and I say, 'exclusive.' Remote? Perhaps. But I prefer *exotic*. Harsh? Maybe to some. I like to say *rustic*. Even pure. Unspoiled. Private."

The landscapes faded away and images of executives began to scroll by, most looking harried and anxious. They had the exaggerated emotional frustration of actors in infomercials.

"Now I'm sure I don't have to tell you how hard it is for the modern business man, or person, pardon me miss Randi, to get away from it all. Smart phones, wireless laptop access at the beach. The temptation is always there to turn a vacation into telecommuting. The demands on the business executive are inescapable, I think you'd agree."

"Positively, yes." Pontius made a big show of nodding. "I am all too familiar," he said eagerly.

"Well, I think, then, you'll all appreciate the opportunity we saw. It was a perfect storm—our relationship with foreign, some say rogue, governments. The latitude with which we operate. A nation chock full with stressed out CEOs, captains of capitalism on their last nerve. The relentless pressure from stockholders. Then there's the expertise of my… staff. Our background in overcoming sophisticated security details. Is a 'vacation from it all' even possible, I ask you?"

"Assuredly not," Pontius said.

"Bingo. The market is ready for an enforced leisure services provider." Mr. Z stabbed his controller at the screen a third time, and a video began, mute surveillance footage through a fiber optic fish-eye lens. An Asian man hunched forward in a high-backed, ergonomic chair, furiously shouting into a phone like a silent film star. The man's attention shifted abruptly off screen. The source of his shock became apparent as a team of hooded, armed men swarmed him, tasered him, bagged his head, and bound his hands behind his back. He thrashed like a farm animal as they hoisted him aloft and bum-rushed him from the office. His phone dangled limply on its cord. His desk chair was still spinning as the strike team disappeared.

"Holy shit," Chet Wallace said. "That took, like, less than ten seconds."

Mr Z. smiled proudly.

"Now how about it? Was that a state-sponsored kidnapping? Hardly! That's actual footage from one of our beta test clients. We'll call him Mr. Wang. He's at the head of a major software-as-service provider in Silicon Valley. Six months before this footage was taken, Wang paid us handsomely for our P.O.W. package—that's *Prisoner of 'WOW!'*. Guy like that spends eighteen hours a day on the job. Forced to make multimillion dollar decisions in a split second. Hadn't had a vacation in ten years. But after he paid our deposit, every day was full of joyous anticipation. He didn't know when we were coming. Complete surprise. Every day he was driven to work, he didn't know if that day would be the day we would storm his office. Didn't know if that would be the day his driver called in sick and the service would send one of our replacement drivers to whisk him away. Let me tell you, he was alive like never before. After that rendition, we *entertained* Wang for six weeks. You think he was checking email? Ho, ho, no *sir*."

"Rendition and torture truly are semantic conditions," Randi said. "There's transformative potential in shifting perspectives."

"I imagine it can be very therapeutic for an executive to be forced to relinquish control," Pontius said.

"Affirmative," Mr. Z said. "But that's just one side of the model as far as we see it. For some of our clients, there's a deep desire to exercise a *greater* degree of control. Total control, even. If you'll permit me, I'd like to show the footage one more time."

Mr. Z replayed the footage, stopping it at the key moment when they bagged Wang's head.

"The operative you see masking the client in this shot is not, in fact, one of our operatives. That's a colleague of Mr. Wang's, the head of a semi-conductor importer in Oakland. Guys used to play golf together, prior to the ceaseless demands of their high pressure careers. Let's call him Mr. Leland. Well, Mr. Leland purchased our *Soldier of Fortune 500* package. For six weeks, he was intimately involved in our team's... *entertaining* of Mr. Wang."

The video screen clicked off.

"As you can see, we have a very lucrative model. Clients on both sides of the experience. But we have one problem."

"The problem is growth, expanding your presence in the marketplace," Pontius said.

"Roger that," Mr. Z said, taking his seat at the head of the table. "That's where we face a challenge. We're the category leader... hell, category *inventor*. But we need a partner that can help us identify new clients and how to spread the word to those clients. You can't exactly take out a Superbowl ad for this, am I right?"

"This could be a powerful opportunity for a viral online play," Randi said. "Intrigue. Password protected websites. Surveillance videos on YouTube. We could leverage conspiracy theorist groups on social media platforms to maximize distribution."

"Yes, yes," Pontius said. "I couldn't agree *more*. But there needs to be a personal component. Something like a black-tie invitation. I know this set very well—you have to appeal to their sense of luxury expectations. Bespoke work, for sure."

"P.J., that's why we need you. I may know where to shock a man so his bowels let loose on my order, but I'm afraid I'm a little out of my field on getting the word out to the jet set." Mr. Z withdrew a cigar from his jacket and took his time cutting and lighting it. He offered one to Pontius, who took it and put it in his own jacket pocket. The bitter smoke gave volume to the golden overhead lighting. The cigar bestowed upon Mr. Z an air of cold war philosopher.

"Follow me here. I am willing to know what I don't know. I know that in our business of the unknown, we don't know how to make ourselves known, so you must know how to make our unknowns known to the knowers we need to know. So know and appreciate this: It's a real leap for me to trust your instincts on what *you* know."

"Ye-e-e-ssss," Pontius said slowly. "There is that."

Mr. Z leaned forward, his hands folded before him on the table.

"What I can definitely appreciate is your willingness to perform hands-on research. No one else has proposed going the extra mile to get intimately acquainted with our business."

Whatever presentation Chet had been reamed over, it seemed superfluous at this point. I watched Randi's eyes meet Pontius' eyes, and understood that more was in play than a piece of business.

"So unless you can see any reason to delay?" Mr. Z asked.

Pontius shook his head, no. "I believe we are ready to get started immediately..." he licked his lips, "on the *deep dive*."

On the phrase *deep dive*, a scene virtually identical to the one we had just watched on the video screen unfolded in Mr. Z's war room. Had I been the intended target, I feel certain I would have been just as oblivious as Chet Wallace was when the Rendition Vacations operatives swept in and tagged and bagged him. The tasering was not strictly necessary (and might have spared us all from the final noxious assault Chet's body let loose), but I had the sense that Pontius wanted to see his imagined mole twitch and suffer under the guise of bonafide client research. Chet treated us to a medley of barnyard noises as they hauled him from the room. Randi deferred her attention to her BlackBerry as Pontius looked on with a bemused half-smile, thinking he had just dealt a mortal blow to the shadowy Canard Consulting, the very existence of which I was beginning to doubt.

"In twelve weeks, he'll have a thorough understanding of our service," Mr. Z said, when the room was still again.

Mr. Z escorted us to a freight elevator. We were brought to the surface to watch Mr. Z's goons manhandle Chet Wallace into the charter jet, engines already whining on the tarmac. The running lights flashed red and white as the pilot performed his final checks. In a minute or so, the jet had taxied and departed, leaving a light brown haze of exhaust behind as it climbed and banked sharply. It disappeared into the low comforter of clouds. Where Chet landed and how he was entertained was privileged information.

We climbed into the waiting helicopter to be flown back to McCarran International. The pilot treated us to a sightseeing fly-over of the Strip before dropping us off. I would never see Las Vegas the same way again, and in truth, the desire to ever return had been dimmed by the vision of my father's ghost bellowing at me, legs akimbo above the crowded roulette table in the Golden Nugget. What he had said was still on me, just as the smell of the casino permeated everything.

Randi barely made her flight back to New York, but as it would happen, Pontius and I had unstructured time in the airport together. Instead of flying back to Atlanta, he was destined for Cleveland on mysterious business, irked to be booked on a Southwest cattle tube without first class.

Pontius charged down the concourse, one hand clasped to his roller bag, the other balled in a tiny fist, swinging as though planting and lifting a hiking pole. He was still ruffled from security. One flap of his suit jacket tucked into the seat of his pants, the other bunched over the holster of his BlackBerry. Cold drafts poured from the vents, but his forehead and upper lip prickled with glossy particles of sweat. He arrived at Gate C9, the desk empty.

He wasn't used to arriving early. We had enough time for a good dinner somewhere in one of the labyrinthine casinos a fifteen minute cab ride away, but neither one of us had the nerve to face the supernova again. The neon and noise of McCarran's C Terminal was garish enough. Invisible studio audiences, their voices eternally disembodied, chanted *Wheel! Of! Fortune!* from the tinny megawatt speakers in the slot machines.

Pontius unhooked his BlackBerry and fondled the thumbwheel. His light was green, a condition which seemed to provoke the reaction I had when mine was red. He jammed it home again.

"Well!" Pontius huffed. He pushed his glasses into the furrow atop his nose. "I suppose we have a little idle time."

"A drink?"

"I think we could do with a meal," he said. He lengthened his neck and gave a groundhog survey of what was available. "I've been-meaning to sit down and conference with you a bit, Nick. If only... we had a suitable—*ah!* Most excellent."

He set off in the direction of the center food court, pumping his way through a stone-tiled boxing ring of fast-food counters shouldered so tight they were all hybrids of a sort, a moribund Sbarro's doubling as a breakfast buffet, the Burger King doling out foil-wrapped tacos from a lower chute. A single row of dripping soda teats served the fast food banks from a sticky stainless steel bar in a dark corner. Vegas' regurgitated tourists bumped and shuffled along the metal queues, waxy pale in the high-efficiency cannons of overhead light. Pontius' gaze locked onto the Cold Stone Creamery.

The clerk plopped a heavy wedge of rocky road ice cream onto the flat marble and worked it with two flat-edged dough knives, the light flickering in Pontius' tiny, octagonal lenses.

"Nick, you're doing top-flight consulting work," Pontius said. "It's evident that your mind is as suited for this as mine is. I recognize it in you. It is a calling."

The clerk scraped and swooped the mass of ice cream into a bucket on a digital scale. The skeletal digits danced from the row of zeroes.

"A bit of red velvet now," Pontius pointed a knuckle at the case, tucking his chin into his collar. "If it's fresh."

The clerk rolled his prison-thick forearms in tight orbits, rippling the Bic-blue script. He dipped and wiped the block blades and peeled up a rind of lung-colored ice cream.

"Now, if anything, I think you are modest about your talents... and dare I say, *passion* for the firm? I don't invest in this 'outside the box' thinking that's bandied about so much. In my experience, this business is not at all about getting outside of the box, but *expanding the capacities of the box*."

Hack, hack, hack, the clerk chopped and whipped the blob on the brick. He dropped it in the bucket atop the nugget-flecked rocky road.

"You want two spoons?" he asked.

"No, wait now," Pontius said. "Just a *dollop* now of cake batter."

The clerk peeled and scraped a cortical mass of buttermilk on top of the pile, skipping the show on the slab. The bucket of sweet offal weighed in at $33.67.

"So what do you say?" Pontius asked. "How much larger should we make the box?"

"I don't follow," I said. Pontius stuck his finger in the bucket and dredged up a finger's worth of the cake batter.

"Staphh," he bubbled, the upper ridge of his lip crested with melted ice cream. "Expansion of the San Francisco office. Building the West Coast *team*."

The clerk stood idle, rectangle blade dripping onto the slab.

"There would be a promotion, of course. To SVP. A bit more day-to-day involvement, but such is the mantle of the senior executive."

"What about you?" the clerk asked. Pontius' head swiveled from my face—I would have been hard pressed to tell you what shape it was in, given my entire head had gone numb—and gaped at the clerk.

"Toppings!" he shouted. "Don't they teach you the process here?" His nostrils flared and he gave a little shake of the head.

"I can see you're overwhelmed, Nick. Clearly, anyone would be. You deserve this, though, so don't hesitate to seize the green field. I'm in this for the very long game, but there will come a time when someone will have to be in line to carry forward the legacy of all we've built."

I could see something like a wormhole opening up in San Francisco, a black portal under the Tantamount Building, the Atlanta horde clawing over the lip, the glimpse of a rosy ape's ass reflected in the polished lobby elevators.

I realized I couldn't hear. The whole terminal had gone silent as Pontius directed the clerk through the final sprinkling.

I stood very still and waved off the clerk when Pontius had paid and tucked his bucket in the crook of his arm. He dug in, spoon in one fist, the little mirror of the BlackBerry in the other. I rode out the wave of panic and tried to remember how the making of a promise was the same as fulfilling the promise in Pontius' world. He seemed not to notice that I'd skipped dinner.

By the end of his bucket, Pontius' glow began to fade. It was not hard to tell a kind of post-drama depression had begun to settle on his shoulders, that his mind rapidly reanimated the specter of Canard again. Late tonight he would murmur his concerns into Shelby's furry shoulder. Randi would exercise the AMEX and purge the stink of everything not-New York from her body with a detoxifying wrap and deep tissue massage. And I would return to the foggy, self-interested Garden of Eden, and bask in the sunshine of my suicide bomber once again.

Chapter 9

Nick's Evening of Public Poetry, Private Fashion, & an Uncovered Secret

September and October are said to be the most gorgeous months in San Francisco. The rains aren't in yet, the summer fogs have thinned, and the planet tilts so the light is gold and rich with the atmosphere of formative time and a future nostalgia. Flowing into the dusk river of red brake lights on the 101 approaching the Seventh street exit, the city worked its Fall magic on me. My itinerary for the next twenty-four hours was my own. Jake Hawkins was reading at The Lone Palm on 22nd and Guerrero to celebrate the release of his new chapbook, *Restricted Airspace*. For the rest of the night, I had Sadie to myself, and I intended to forget LaBar Partners Limited for at least twelve hours.

I made it twelve minutes. The front desk at the Tantamount presented me with an overnight FedEx box. It contained my pre-charged, pre-configured, brand new BlackBerry. Its red eye pulsed immediately upon powering up. I scrolled through the messages, the chain of red exclamation marks next to each of Randi's and Pontius'. In the elevator, one email to the entire firm caught my attention:

To: LaBar Partners Limited <execs@labarpartnerslimited.com>
From: Pontius J. LaBar <pjlabar@labarpartnerslimited.com>
Subject: RETREAT UPDATE & other news

In response to recent biz dev setbacks and in anticipation of temporary cash flow issues, we have relocated the December company retreat to the Embassy-Suites in Midtown Atlanta.

It is with deep regret that I cannot, in good conscience, extend an open invitation to spouses and partners. It will also be one day shorter (we have elected to forego the awards ceremony).

I assure you the Embassy-Suites is a world-class conference space with the amenities you all deserve after a challenging, but still tremendously successful year thus far.

Still anticipating extraordinary team building,
PJL

P.S. We are reducing all non-senior executive compensation packages by 20% effective immediately.

Of course Rendition Vacations was not the magic remedy for LaBar Partners Limited's dwindling income and astronomical expenses. Whatever motherlode Randi and Pontius had imagined was not there, and though the firm was paid for Chet Wallace's "field research"vacation, the fees were offset by hard costs that Mr. Z's people incurred for Chet's time abroad, per the ill-negotiated agreement.

The clock was running now. You could hear the stall warning in the LaBar Partners Limited cockpit. The dive wasn't far behind. The twenty percent pay cut meant myself, Ono Anna, Mackie Wallace and theoretically Chet Wallace (if a mole could be compensated while entertained in a Burmese pit cell). I would worry about it later. As long as I didn't receive an urgent call for a Monday morning meeting in another godforsaken midwestern city, I didn't care. As the money went, so went the gravitational pull of the work, so transformed the golden handcuffs to less precious metals.

Sadie had the large table in the living room covered with soldering irons, diagrams, various disassembled iPods, wiring harnesses, small green sandwich circuit boards, batteries, and an array of key fobs. She was wearing a jeweler's hood, which made her eyes appear massive and owl-like when she turned to greet me.

"Weary explorer," she said. "What tales of depravity have you to share with me?"

"You wouldn't believe me if I told you."

She stood up, wearing her underwear and a white tank-top, no bra. Tattooed names and logos of defense contractors hugged the tops of her thighs like inky garters. I pointed.

"How lucky to be... Lockheed Martin and... Northrop Grumman?"

"How lucky to be Nick Bray," she said and crossed the room.

"Getting luckier by the minute." She felt so warm and slight, it was hard to imagine parts of her accelerated past the speed of sound.

"Do you want to see the jacket?" she asked.

"How about later," I said. "Try it on for me later."

"Are you sure? You're the only person I can show it to. I want to show it to you."

"Yeah, I'm sure. Later."

She rubbed her forehead on my chest. I touched the back of her neck where I knew the Apple logo was.

"You know, sometimes it's not as easy for me as it seems to be for you," I said.

She looked up at me. I motioned to the disassembled electronics strewn across the table. "All of this. It would be OK with me if maybe it wasn't so... present? Have you ever thought that maybe this isn't such—"

"Don't say it, Nick. Don't ask me. You can't ask me."

I could see the threat was real. If I asked her not to go through with it, she would disappear.

"This is not easy for me," she said. She took a step back. "But you make it easier. So don't fuck that up, OK?"

Love. Two people holding guns to each other's heads.

The Lone Palm, with its round tables draped in white cloth and ubiquitous blue lighting, resembled a shabby refugee of the supper club heyday, a bygone era appropriated a few days past its sell by date. This was precisely the effect the owners wanted. Miniature silver bowls with snack mix lay scattered about, and behind the tiny, triangular corner stage, a stenciled palm tree curved beneath the ceiling. A microphone perched at the top of its black stand like an emaciated raven.

Jake Hawkins sat at a table down front wearing his TSA uniform. He hadn't worn it for ironic effect, but had in fact come straight from work at SFO to the Lone Palm. Had I known we were both leaving the airport so close together, I would have given him a lift in the car service so he would have had time to change. His beard seemed fuller than when I saw him last on my pass through security. The club was not at all crowded yet, and I had the impression that only a handful of the people there were specifically there to hear Jake read. The rest were neighborhood locals who would probably leave once Jake took the stage.

He seemed genuinely touched that we made it to the club. He signed me a copy of his new book, the pages hand stitched flight sickness bags, so the book opened like a great accordion, poems aligned like tiny instructions. I bought us all a round of drinks. I talked about my trip. We drank a second round. The bar was beginning to fill, and Jake introduced me to a number of his friends, mostly poets and musicians from the city.

Each introduction made me feel a little more transparent, as though the painters, writers, musicians, and poets could see and sum up the con that was my life, and politely let it go by not asking me what it was I did. These people did not ask you what you did for a living—they wanted to know what you did to live. They all (and this included Sadie) were somehow brighter and less anxious than the Monday morning crowd I shared rows with in airplanes.

Time passed, the bar grew full. Sadie guarded our front row table as I brought back more booze. Each trip I returned to find another flannel shirted kid asking her about her tattoos. They saw but a fraction of the whole, though they admired what they saw. I washed up on the table again like a dim-witted cousin or uncle, and the look on most of their faces asked the same question: *This guy?*

Finally, someone took the stage to introduce Jake. There were inside jokes, references to poems, to self-destructive nights. We were all a little drunk, but not sloppy. Some people whooped when Jake's big frame took the stage. He really was an enormous guy, a great golem of poetry and x-ray operation with his hunched shoulders and black beard. He was a minor deity for some of these people. He was anonymous for the majority. He was among people who cared, even deep in their surreal couplets, about how one word rubbed against the next.

What I loved about him, and what I loved about all of these people who made me feel like such a fraud, was the way they suggested by their effort that maybe the musicians on the deck of the Titanic were not cheap metaphors for futility and an unwillingness to face the fact of the freezing water as it rose. They were makers, fully aware of their making in the certainty of death. Some were running from it, some were walking towards it, and these people, Jake's people, were dancing on the way. Even as the city pecked at their livers. Because everyone was going to cover the distance one way or another.

When he was done reading, Jake signed a few more copies, sold a couple, but gave the rest of them away. Some departed for pinball and photo booths in other bars. There was a party carrying on somewhere else that we were invited to, but we parted company with Jake by the curb. We walked a few blocks until the taxis began to emerge on Valencia, interested again in fares.

Sadie kissed me in the back of the cab, and I let her, then I kissed her back. Momentarily I was not Nick.

We stumbled through the bright light of the Tantamount lobby and into the elevator. I could feel that we were accelerating upward and at the same time hurling towards an event, the way that an evening passes a point and begins to take you with it, to sweep you in it's inevitable undertow. Though the apartment was dark, the ambient light of the elevated city revealed the contours and surfaces in a starlight-like halftone.

"I want to show you my jacket," Sadie said, and she sounded considerably more drunk that I had thought she was. She pushed me into one of the Eames chairs. I went down heavy. She disappeared into the back bedroom and was gone for a while, and I began to feel, through the overriding electric thrill of kissing her, a gnawing guilt work its way into my stomach. This was not how it should be. The electronics scattered on the table looked like a scale model of a bombed out Japanese city. I felt like I was taking advantage.

I may have dozed a minute. The light from the hallway cut my eyes and was gone. I could see her figure walking towards the living room, a kind of iridescence at her edges, like fuel shining on the night's pavement. She stepped into the twilight living room wearing a large, blue ski parka and nothing else. The jacket's neck was ringed with a high sheep's fur collar. The bulky parka covered her breasts, but not the map of tattooed logos over her stomach. She was completely naked from the waist down, the puffed bottom edge of the jacket stopping mid-thigh at the names of the defense contractors. Shadows crossed between her legs, and she turned slowly, a little unsteadily, so I could see that her red hair spilled in a tarnish over the back of the fur collar. She turned to face me again and walked forward, her hands pushed into the side pockets.

"It looks remarkably like a jacket," I said, my own voice sounding remote.

When she was but a few feet from me, close enough that I could lean forward and touch her with the palm of my hand, she swept her hands up, and the liner of the jacket separated into a vast, ribbed bat's wing, and underneath the tidy bricks of plastic explosives swung heavily; coils of wire branching arteries and veins of the jacket's terrible and many chambered heart. She was positively beaming, her whole body exposed, breasts white and small once revealed.

I did lean forward, the image of her at once insect and angel, and I gripped one of the bricks of plastic explosive in its pouch. I took a brick from the opposite wing of the jacket in my other palm and dragged my thumb across it—it was smooth and cool and felt somewhat damp. I was close enough to her stomach now that I could feel my breath hitting her skin. She gazed down at the top of my head. Her mouth was open a bit, and then she smiled.

"Nick Bray, are you touching my Semtex?" she murmured.

"I am," I said, looking down at the curve of her belly. These were the compounds that would awake and split the dream of her into a hundred thousand particles. They slept and waited with pornographic indifference. They waited for the detonator's directorial touch and their innate chemical reactions to cascade. There was a composite smell, her own odor rising from her body and the strange graphite deathly smell of the electronics and the plastic explosives. It was not unpleasant, this upholstery and plastic draft of new car. I slid my hands from the heavy, firm bricks and onto her hips. I pushed my face against her stomach and she rested her hands on the top of my head. I turned my head and pressed my ear to her and listened to her blood commuting through the invisible passageways of her body, where I wanted it to stay.

"I think this jacket might get in the way," she said and took her hands from my head. She stepped back and shrugged the heavy coat from her shoulders and hung it on the back of the other chair. She was bare, save the logos marking the contour map of her body. She turned and walked towards the bedroom. It had been so very long since anything like this had happened.

"I'll be right there," I called into the dark hallway. "Bathroom," I said in her absence, though she hadn't asked a thing. She was waiting.

I bumbled in the pitch dark of the bathroom, aware that my flummoxed, drunken reflection was waiting for me to flick on the light and lay bare, in noxious fluorescent light, all of the pale, flabby outward signs that marked me as a spiritually bankrupt wretch. What I did not expect, however, was Dr. Michael W. Bray seated high and legless once again on the commode.

"Hot damn," he said. "It's about time."

"Jesus! What are you *doing* here?"

"I wanted to apologize. I lost myself a little the last time we met." He waggled his wolfish brows. "Should I come back later?"

"What do you think?"

"It's about time it happened for you and her. I mean, not that I would care, but I was beginning to wonder… you're are a young man living in San Francisco… but now, finally, the show is getting good here. Your ratings are way up."

"Well, bad news for you: Nothing's going to happen," I said.

"Oh, is that so? Is it every night you ply a beautiful, young girl with poetry and alcohol so you can come home and rub one out in the sink?"

"Who *are* you? Anyway, it's not right," I said. "I shouldn't do this. She's too young. She's probably drunk. It'll change everything between us."

"Son, please—are there not enough women in this world hesitating to screw you? Why volunteer for the cause?"

"I fully realize you might not recognize self-restraint, Dr. Bray."

"Oh goody. Here comes that high ground you've always loved."

"Just because a new batch of undergrads... *unfurled* themselves for you each semester didn't mean you had to peel the panties off each one."

"Bah. You overstate the case. So I wasn't a saint, this is true, but who cares now?"

"Me. Still. You should have cared then."

"Spare me. Has it ever occurred to you you might overestimate your importance in this little transaction between yourself and Girl Dynamite back there? Who are you, Nick Bray the big bad wolf? Maybe *you're* Little Red Riding Hood. What makes you think you're even capable of taking advantage of her?"

"She's young? She's drunk?"

"*You're* young. *You're* drunk. And you're both lonesome as hell. And has it occurred to you she loves you?"

"I don't believe that."

"Oh, here we go. Because she's not looking for happily ever after? How long do you think you have? Son, sometimes the short run is as good as it gets. All of this you think you know, this absolute right and wrong of yours. It's like money after the apocalypse. It isn't worth shit."

"I'm going to turn off the lights. When I turn them back on, it'd be best if you weren't here."

"Okey-dokey. Time to put Genie Dad back in the bottle."

I turned off the light. The room was womb pitch, but I could tell he was still there.

"There's a black wind blowing in the cotton field, son. There's no bed of clouds and pitchers of ambrosia waiting for you over here. Remember I warned you. I've said my piece."

I turned on the light and he was gone.

I picked my way back to Sadie's room, where I found her naked and asleep on the sheets. She was curled in a ball, and I could see the dark patch of the American Airlines logo spanning the little muscled valley of her lower back. I pulled the comforter over her, then fetched a glass of tap water from the kitchen and placed it on the table beside the bed. I imagined her at eighty, all of these bright and defiant logos degraded into stretched and creased battlefield maps of blue and purple. I imagined her at my age on the other side of a prison plexiglass window, still unwilling to pick up the receiver.

I closed the door and returned to the living room. My BlackBerry's eye burned red among the disemboweled electronics on the dining room table, and it pleased me to imagine it could sense dismembered relatives nearby. I lifted Sadie's bomb jacket from the back of the chair and wore it over my shoulders like a shawl, to feel the pouches of plastic explosive against my own body. It was cold and and heavy and I decided I did not like it.

I turned my back on Sadie's workshop and sat in the Eames' lounge chair with my laptop. I had no intention of checking my email, but the computer in the lap was a good defense against extended meditation on the imponderable. When it occurred to me to type in Sadie's brother's name, I'm not sure. But I began pulling on the thread, asking Google questions with quotation marks and plus signs, mixing in Afghanistan and IED.

But IED turned out to be the wrong acronym. The defining one turned out to be PTSD. The subject of the article was untreated Post-Traumatic Stress Disorder and the year-over-year rise in active duty suicides.

Sgt. Anthony J. Parrish of Denver, CO, age 33, dead of a self-inflicted gunshot wound while guarding terrorists in Kandahar.

No roadside bombs, no remote trigger men. The trigger man was the victim.

Chapter 10

In Which the Intimation of a Celebrity Client Whips LaBar Partners Limited into a Frenzy, & Ill Decisions are Made

In the galaxy of Pontius' desires, no constellation shone brighter than his undying dream of fame. Though his firm had earned him considerable personal wealth, he remained unknown beyond the kingdom of his serfs, and their loyalty (or willingness to till field in the magic kingdom) depended entirely on his capability to purchase it. Therefore he was no king.

No one seated him in a restaurant ahead of a crowd of reservations. No one took his picture from a phalanx of scootering paparazzi. Yes, he drove the entry level sports cars of the class, but they were not given to him as gifts from studio executives, sports stars, or titans of media. He purchased them, the expense of which gradually eroded his control over others.

When he awoke at 3AM with hunger, he did not summon a personal butler by bedside buzzer, but lumbered naked to his own refrigerator where he fumbled with a block of Costco cheddar and a box of Carr's table crackers. Never did his lack of fame strike him greater than during his midnight hour battle with obscurity, when his long-unseen genitals wiggled south as he grunted over the cold, hard cheese with the dull knife.

At times, the lack was so acute that he would dress in the middle of the night and drive to the office, where he would hold conference with Shelby, his constant and wordless companion.

Each week, Mackie Wallace collected copies of *US Weekly*, *People*, and *STAR* from the local convenience stores and hid them inside the pink pages of the *Financial Times* for delivery to Pontius' office. We knew, at dire hours when our proposals and presentations lay rotting in his inbox, waiting for his review, he was enclosed in his penthouse Watching Porsche, diligently tracking the stock of celebrities. The charade of secrecy was something of a mystery, because given a chance, he pontificated on the power dynamics of celebrity relationships as eagerly as analysts who reviewed the mergers and acquisitions of multinational corporations. In a file on his BlackBerry, he collected and invented the hybrid names of couples, in the tradition of *Brangelina*. He savored most the fiery breakup of a celebrity whose career disintegrated upon re-entry into the common public.

Yet no single feature irked him more than the *They're Just Like Us!* candid shots of celebrities caught in pedestrian moments, such as waiting in line to buy a carton of fat-free Greek yogurt or unloading a baby stroller from a Bugatti. While the complete collapse of a celebrity's esteem entertained him, with those who were still revered, he preferred to believe in the unbroken continuum of their exclusion from the commonplace, as a fantasizing teenager does, having never been a celebrity. He instructed Mackie to razor out these features from the magazine before they were delivered to his office.

Pontius wanted his name to fall from celebrities' mouths, just as theirs fell from his. So it was in the pursuit of fame that LaBar Partners Limited became speculatively focused on one famous client: Shaun D. Braun, NFL running back and golden boy #1 on speed dial with a hundred Hollywood stars and New York hip hop moguls.

Shaun D. Braun had yet to blossom into the fashion-designing, foundation-founding, cologne-branding domain of his pro sports set, but all signs pointed that way. All of the ingredients were there; the hard-knock poverty beginnings, the absent parents replaced by ahickory paddle grandmother, the coach who spotted young Shaun's talent when he was a fleet-footed Pop Warner kid in too-small shoes, the impeccable high and state school seasons, the teflon deflection of moral corruption, the early draft, the record-breaking contract, maintaining the Sunday morning visits to his grandmother's house to escort her to church, the elevation of his old posse into the high-paid ranks of a pro-sports entourage, and finally the attention of that infamous army of single-initialed rap stars—the P. this and R. that and chorus of Lil's.

All of this was bolstered by superhuman feats on the field and an uncommonly humble "you play the game, but don't let the game play you" demeanor in front of the media machine. Reporters lost their nerve. His public persona disarmed them, and whatever rumors they had sharpened to bring to the interview dulled and tarnished in their quivers. He was one film cameo with Jack Nicholson and Morgan Freeman away from a blinding fame supernova.

Which is why it was hard to believe the email I received, summoning me back to Atlanta for emergency business development meetings with the pigskin gladiator, Shaun D. Braun. I called Randi Bevelecazzo in New York immediately after receiving the message, as it was precisely the sort of firm-wide announcement which I thought would signal the beginning of Pontius' total mental breakdown. But the email turned out to be true.

The contact had come by way of her husband, black arts magician of sports reputation damage control, Donald "D.B." Bellamy (she kept her own last name in the marriage for professional reasons). Word had come that Shaun D. Braun was preparing to launch his first major project beyond the NFL, and he was looking for a partner to advise him on "brand positioning and messaging."

In fact, the referral came from Bellamy's old friend from his broadcasting days (Shaun D. Braun's current personal advisor), Major Washington. Major sought a partner on Shaun's behalf. Major was not so named for a previously held military rank as he was self-christened prior to his broadcasting career. He was known as "The Major" to Shaun and most everyone in the world of pro sports.

No word had come down yet as to the precise nature of Shaun's venture.

In retrospect, the setup seems pretty clear. Maybe Major Washington had tried to dissuade Shaun from his business idea, and Shaun had gone against him. Though Major had been the architect behind Shaun's carefully chosen post-game interview words, the associations with celebrities, the "good son" visits back to his old neighborhood, Shaun may have decided to buck the savvy old broadcaster's yoke. Never mind that apart from the raw instincts Shaun possessed on the field, everything about Shaun D. Braun's image was the direct result of Major Washington's council. So when Shaun tells him he's going ahead with his big play regardless of Major's advice, Major picks up the phone and calls Randi's husband, D.B., because there's no dissuading the kid.

And Major was right, of course. This idea Shaun had was an immediate career killer, and if he was really set on it, the only thing to do was to rush him into it as fast as possible, get D.B. to handle the damage control when it all went down (with a not-so-inconsiderable kickback to Major for the referral), and commence the slow rehabilitation of Shaun's celebrity equity, which Major knew was still of considerable value as a long-term investment. As a media commodity, the fall from and return to grace could conceivably increase Shaun's appreciation over time.

It was not hard to imagine the phone call, Major Washington sipping a scotch on the veranda of his modest Inman Park house, enjoying the first cool fall evening, dialing D.B.'s phone number. *How's Randi, how's your work going?* He explains Shaun D. Braun's position and his situation. *Here's the thing, D.B., the only thing I'm missing is an accelerant for bad fucking ideas.*

And then D.B., who had long since reached his breaking point with his wife's incessant, senseless rambling over mediocre hotel room service about "the necessity we speak in tones of innovation" and "the media paradigm is in a state of vocal revision" sees one of those two-birds-and-one-big-stone moments.

So, Major, why don't we keep it in the family? I know just the firm for you.

Enter LaBar Partners Limited.

I arrived in the Atlanta office to find Mackie Wallace sorting through a large stack of receipts behind the reception desk. Rogue hairs frayed from her shellacked head. I wondered how she was taking Chet's rendition, or if she had helped engineer it. As she sorted the receipts into piles, she tapped out figures on a large calculator, the antiquated type with a ribbon of white paper scrolling from the top. She barely looked up when I walked in the door.

Further down the hallway, I observed two men and a woman sitting in the conference room. It took no time at all to understand they were from an ad agency. The one that looked like a cross between a Devo tribute band member and a refugee from Dachau was the creative director. He was engaged in picking lint from the arm of his Jobsian turtleneck. The other two, a man and a woman, were the account executive and the copywriter. Discerning which was which was difficult, but I was leaning towards the woman as the copywriter and the man as the account exec, simply because I figured she was the one the creative director would prefer to fuck.

A word here about consultants and agencies. From time to time we met with ad agencies. They reviled us. Pontius defaced their work while producing none of his own, and when he had the ear of one of their clients, he could occasionally make the agency seem like such idiots that the trade pubs would report a change in the agency of record for the client within a week.

In meetings, ad agency teams were a lot like golden retriever puppies, endearingly witless in their unconditional love of their master and wholly absorbed in the twee acts of narcissistic ass-sniffing, tussling with their own ideas, snapping at criticism with little razor teeth, and humping each other's heads to clarify internal agency politics. When they failed at that, they graduated to a brand management consultancy. What they were doing in the Atlanta office, I couldn't fathom. I slipped back to the receptionist's desk.

"Mackie, what's with the group in the conference room?"

She looked up momentarily from her receipts, wide eyed. "Do they need water?"

"No. Why are they *here?*"

"Mr. LaBar is hiring an agency to help with the spec work for Shaun D. Braun. They're here to pitch."

"*Hiring?* We're hiring an agency? Is the PowerPoint beyond Ono's capabilities this time?"

"Ono's not going to work with this client. Mr. LaBar doesn't think she'd be a good fit."

She tapped at the calculator and a fresh inch of paper sprung from the machine. Her smile crept further up her skull.

"Something wrong?"

"No, no. Just adding up these expense receipts from Mr. LaBar."

It was a well known fact that when Pontius became aroused at the prospect of a new client, he went into a spending frenzy. The categories of "mandatory expenditures" included haircuts, massages, and grooming to help him "decompress" prior to the upcoming meetings, "bespoke wardrobe updates" to best present an "executive of his standing," two to four days run-up and run-down from the meeting in the closest five-star resort for "intense personal planning," a complete technological update of his BlackBerry and laptop, and a large cash disbursement to cover "incidental necessities" during travel. If, for a meeting with a client like Rendition Vacations, he had incurred preparatory expenses in the neighborhood of $45,000, I could not estimate how much he was burning prior to a meeting with a celebrity client. The ad agency was a symptom of the magnitude of the disease, though.

We all sat through four presentations, each interchangeable with the one before it: An account executive without the stomach for straight-up prostitution, a copywriter without the chops or balls for stand up comedy who spent half the meeting daydreaming about the screenplay he had been writing since sophomore undergrad, and a creative director who placed the import of his portfolio somewhere between Hitchcock and Michelangelo.

They were all moderately proficient in bullshitese, but they were equally unprepared for Randi's doctorate in the field. When one of the creative directors mistakenly engaged in an argument with Randi rather than nodding and politely waiting for her oxygen to run out, she dropped conjunctions entirely and unloaded a Tourettic volley of jargon and adverbs.

Pontius openly heckled the portfolio pieces he didn't like. When one appeared that he did like, he became so infuriated he hadn't thought of the idea that he pursed his lips and simply said "Next, now." During the third presentation, he asked Mackie to bring him a box of Little Debbie devil cakes.

Ono spent the meeting sketching chihuahuas on her note pad. Her actual chihuahua sat in her office dressed in a miniature Ralph Lauren rugby-inspired sweater. Periodically its yaps could be heard in the conference room, causing Ono to make a small *squee* noise. At every opportunity she sprung up and hustled to her office. Shelby's conference room curtain remained closed for the meeting. At the conclusion of the pitches, Pontius retired to Shelby's office to hold conference and ponder his decision.

An hour after the pitches, Mackie Wallace summoned me to Pontius' office.

"Nick, I need your candid counsel," Pontius said, his eyes locked on his computer screen. "I think you understand my penchant for detail. Tomorrow night we're going to meet with Shaun D. Braun at his mansion to discuss his business vision."

Pontius put his glasses back on and swiveled his flatscreen to face me. The screen was filled with luxury cars from a dealer who provided fractional ownership for those who couldn't afford to buy.

"Do you think we should arrive in the white-on-white Bentley, or would separate Ferrari's be more his style?"

I knew better than to fight him on it. I just tried to put out of my mind that for what he'd spend on the rentals, six poets from the Lone Palm reading could live for a year.

"I think the only person to see us arrive will be his valet. So one Bentley."

Pontius leaned back in his chair and patted his shirt pocket for the last Little Debbie. He ripped open the package with his teeth.

"But the valet will talk." He narrowed his eyes. "I've been watching rap videos on YouTube all morning, and they haven't really helped narrow it down at all."

"Well, then, I still think the Bentley," I said. "Go for understatement."

Pontius blinked, the Devil Cake rolling in his mouth.

"But hire a driver for it, too," I said.

"Ooooh, yes, yes, brilliant." A paint chip of brown frosting jumped from his lip and tumbled to his pants. "I couldn't agree *more*."

I hadn't confronted Sadie about the story of her brother's death before I left San Francisco. It wasn't as if it changed the validity (or invalidity) of her reasons—if anything, you could argue it might enhance them—but I didn't like that she had lied to me. I thought of all the people she may have told about her brother, I would be the one that got the straight story. The lonesome, angry brother guarding lonesome, murderous men for reasons he can't comprehend decides he'd be better off dead. He's on watch by himself for a few minutes while his buddy goes to the head and his sidearm is close at hand. A split-second decision. No thanks, I've had plenty. Some decisions a long time coming were made with surprising speed.

I thought Sadie could tell me she was furious with him and ashamed of herself for being unable to save him. I thought she could tell me that, sure, her mission was about the war on one level, but on a deeper level it was about having nowhere to store her brother's rejection of her and everyone who loved him. She would paint an airport terminal with it. She would blow out the windows of the Starbucks. She would load herself with wood screws and ball bearings and plastic explosives, one piece of shrapnel for every minute of bewilderment and betrayal she'd felt.

Outside of the Atlantan Terrace Hotel, I spied one of the account executives from the day's meetings. I couldn't remember which agency she'd represented. She was a young, round, pretty Korean girl with red highlights who sucked her cigarette as though trying to reverse the flow of time. By the looks of the ash, she was working through her 7th birthday. She was dressed in her meeting outfit; black skirt, black tights, and a high-collared white shirt open to the tops of her structurally supported breasts. She must have been from the agency in Cincinnati—Porter, Bogusky & Davis or something—the one where I was pretty sure the creative director had eyes for his own French-Canadian copywriter. Normally I would have passed by without saying a word, but I knew what I was doing this particular night.

"Let me guess. You're asking yourself if you can really sleep on the sheets in this shit hole."

She cut me with her eyes until she remembered me from the meeting. That's when her account executive face turned on.

"Oh. My. God. You're so not kidding. I can't *believe* you guys recommend this place, ya know?" She had that North Dakota accent. Adopted. A whiff of missionaries.

"I'll make it up to you," I said. "There's a Hyatt a short taxi ride away. They have a decent bar."

The valet hailed one of Atlanta's saddest minivan taxis into the loop, duct tape holding up the mismatched bumper smile. We piled out at the Hyatt bar. A playerless baby grand piano shone on a raised platform. "Georgia On My Mind" of all things treacled in from speakers in the fake plants.

We drank off four whiskeys fast. It was all a little depressing, because it wasn't as if I had to try very hard. I just alluded to the notion that I was really the one pulling the trigger on RFP. I offered to put her up in a room at the Hyatt for the night on the AMEX.

She had a big, soft bush and no tattoos, and we tussled and probed and tugged and bit and sucked and transacted small abuses and encouraging frictions, but in the end I couldn't get it up. It was not particularly late and I dressed and left while she smoked in the bathroom.

First order of business, a short BlackBerry email to Randi and Pontius:

Cincinnati agency definitely off the list in my professional opinion. NB.

Chapter 11

In Which the Famous Shaun D. Braun Shares His Vision with LaBar Partners Limited

The reasons why Ono Anna had been spared from the Shaun D. Braun meetings became clear the following night when we attended the "meet and greet" house party thrown at his mansion in suburban Atlanta. After passing through a gated guard house a half a mile down, I arrived with Pontius and Randi in the white-on-white-leather Bentley around 9:30 in front of a decidedly modern take on an antebellum mansion. Many classic architectural details were overwhelmed by futuristic add-ons. The fiber optically lit glass brick driveway circled a palatial fountain strobed by fans of lasers. Between the bass frequencies emanating from the house and the light shining through every available window, it seemed as though we were preparing to dock with an enormous Dirty South space station.

The parking area, a two acre covered pavilion, looked like an exotic car show in Frankfurt. At various posts throughout the campus—because you really couldn't call it a yard—stood black-suited men of NFL and/or prison stature whose necks were the circumference of my head. Tight, green topiaries of various football scenes dotted the grass, including huddles and end zone dance celebrations. The whole place cast an afterglow in the sky like a county fair midway, the constellations were completely obscured. There was only one star visible at this address as far as Shaun D. Braun was concerned.

We were lead up the front steps and passed through a pair of metal detectors. A coat and gun check lay just beyond. Security escorted us. Randi Bevelecazzo had been to pro athlete houses in the past with her husband, D.B., as he handled their bountiful image problems. These were usually quiet dinners just before or during calamity, i.e. when most of the contents of the houses had been auctioned to satisfy creditors, or the hours before standing trial for DUI, statutory rape, weapons charges, or all of the above. But even Randi seemed overwhelmed by the foyer of Shaun's mansion. Three stories above the entry, a domed ceiling of linked LCD screens played silent highlight clips of Shaun D. Braun's superhuman plays. His warbling image, engaged in 80 yard returns, touchdowns, and leaping interceptions appeared and disappeared in the gleaming pink marble surfaces that surrounded us on the ground floor. Light of Shaun D. Braun, pools of Shaun D. Braun. The room appeared to be chiseled from a single, solid block.

Pontius must have expected Shaun D. Braun himself to descend the grand staircase like Scarlet O'Hara, and so seemed miffed when Major Washington, D.B.'s friend, emerged from a small pocket door off of the foyer to greet us. Major looked prepared for a court-side interview in his dark charcoal suit with spider silk thin blue pinstripes. He looked like Clarence Thomas, with better eyeglasses, after twelve weeks with a personal trainer. The eyes were the same, though—x-ray capable whirlpools shaded by heavy lids.

"Randi Beve-luh-cazzo," he said, leaning forward to kiss her cheek. "What a pleasure that this worked out." He stepped back and looked at her for a moment longer than was strictly required. When I think about it now, I wonder if Major was looking for some sign of whether or not D.B. had let his own wife in on the larger con, or if he'd kept her in the dark about Major and D.B.'s death and resurrection plans for Shaun.

Randi turned and introduced us to Major.

"My colleagues, Pontius J. LaBar, CEO. From our San Francisco office, Nick Bray."

"As I expected," Major laughed in a practiced way. "If you all looked any stranger you'd be on a leash. Come on now, I'm kidding you." Major reached into his pocket and withdrew three platinum bracelets. They were the type someone else had to clasp to your wrist and close with a jeweler's screwdriver. They smacked a little of expensive handcuffs. I noticed the initials "S.D.B. VIP" engraved on each one. Major affixed them to our wrists one by one.

"These are your access-all-areas passes. They also let security know that you're clear to approach Mr. Braun within arm's length. Please call Mr. Braun 'Mr. Braun' until he asks you *twice* to call him Shaun. Trust me when I say that's what he'll expect, as he'll know I've briefed you on these expectations. You may hear people call him 'D.D.B.' or 'Shay-D,' but under no circumstances are you permitted to use these names. Assume that if you *do* call him by these names, this will be the last time you meet with him. Now if you will all follow me, there's some paperwork we need to take care of before you join the party."

We followed Major through the automatic pocket door in foyer and into his office. It looked and felt like a well-appointed captain's quarters, ringed with photographs of Major's broadcasting career, sports memorabilia, and a few Fender Stratocaster and Les Paul guitars signed in glitzy paint pens. Major stood behind his desk.

"I do not have to explain to you that Mr. Braun's wealth is directly tied to the management of his public image. The non-disclosure agreements you're signing include not only the project you will discuss with Mr. Braun this evening, but everything you see and hear. In fact, you are not permitted to reveal to anyone you are working directly for Mr. Braun, should he decide to hire you. This is not your garden variety NDA, so I urge you to take this with the utmost seriousness."

"Yes, of *course*," Pontius said. "We treat all of our clients with the utmost discretion."

Major took off his glasses and leaned forward on his knuckles.

"Save the bullshit for Mr. Braun, P.J.," Major said. "I am not fucking with you. I saw your prick straining your skivvies when you got out of that rented car. You talk about any of this, it's your mother-fucking ass."

Pontius' face flushed, and his upper lip stuck to his teeth in a peculiar smile he used as the defense most-high against having a tantrum.

"Come on, Major," Randi said. "Come on. Guys. Let's smooth the airspace here. We understand what's in our best interest and Mr. Braun's."

"Very good," Major said. "Now, let's get your man Nick here an escort. Randi, you and Pontius are fine together, but Nick needs someone. Mr. Braun likes to see everyone with someone, and especially someone pretty. It will help you hold his attention. Tell me Nick, do you have a preference?"

"No," I said. "I'm sure anyone you pick is fine."

"It's your call. Dominican? Maybe a little Thai girl, about four-foot-your-belt-line?"

"I trust your judgement."

"Good man. All-righty then." Major snatched the receiver on his desk and punched up an extension. "Hey baby. I'm doing all right. Listen, you got Rosita working tonight? No? What about that Puerto Rican girl, the new one? Kinda short? No, not midget short. What's wrong with you? We don't have any midgets, do we? Well, whatever they're called. Really? Since when? Oh, yeah, yeah, that's right. Because of that one dude from Chicago, what was it? Lil' Mike Mike? Whooee, that was some shit, wasn't it? Like a little Tasmanian devil. Well, good to know. Have to stop by and check her out. Ok, now. Listen, how about send that new Puerto Rican girl down my way. It's on us. No, no, no. No extras. Just arm candy. Yeah, he's about six foot… white guy. Just wearing some Neiman Marcus rack shit, I don't know. Tell her they're VIPs, though."

Major hung up the phone.

"Your girl will be down in a minute. Don't take that shit about the suit personally, Nick. It's a real nice suit. Real sharp."

The question remained: If you had a celebrity client, but couldn't talk about it, did you have a celebrity client at all? Were you in proximity to fame if you couldn't draw attention to your proximity to fame? No matter. Pontius wouldn't be able to keep his mouth shut. Even if Shaun D. Braun decided we weren't the people he needed (but let's face it—this wasn't exactly Shaun's decision to begin with), Pontius would go into the very next meeting running off at the mouth about the "truly exciting work we were engaged in for a certain professional football player." Within two minutes of playing coy about how he couldn't reveal the player, he'd drop Shaun's name.

The Puerto Rican girl was named Asia, and fell under the category of the improbably beautiful. Shaun D. Braun probably picked these girls from clubs and fashion shows as meticulously as San Franciscans did their heirloom tomatoes and organic chard. Being in the same room with her, to say nothing of having her clutching my side, made me feel grotesquely deformed. She was as affectionate as her compensation dictated, which is to say she kept up the appearance of adoration, but I was careful not to reciprocate for fear of the frostbite that awaited me if I crossed the line. Rental Bentleys, rental people.

Perhaps the age of possession and full-time relationships had devolved into a new fractional ownership that better suited our attention spans.

The deeper we traveled into Shaun D. Braun's mansion, the more aware I became of how empty it was, despite a party I could hear raging in the near distance. Wherever it was happening, we were kept away, ferreted through hallways, antechambers and haremesque living rooms, each furnished with an eclectic mix of mismatched pieces, as if individually chosen for price tag rather than aesthetic harmony. It looked like a millionaire's garage sale. If we had been turned loose to find our way out, it's possible we would have been eaten by a Minotaur before making it back to the Bentley. It never occurred to me at the time that we were being led by Major Washington through the empty rooms which protected Shaun D. Braun's inner sanctum from the tidal highs and lows of a perpetual celebrity entourage.

Eventually, we arrived at a regular sort of bedroom door, narrow stained wood with four panels of rounded inner beveling. Major turned and looked each of us in the eye, and then spoke directly to Pontius.

"Remember what I said. Not a word."

Pontius dipped his head. Major knocked softly and leaned against the door frame, like a father listening for noises that might reveal where and what his son was busy hiding.

"Come in," a voice called from inside.

"Not what ya'll expected, is it?" Shaun said.

We stood awkwardly close together in the model of a teenage boy's bedroom. It was not just any teenage boy's bedroom, but an exact replica of Shaun's childhood room from his grandmother's house. A silver and black boom box from the 1980s perched on top of a ramshackle dresser. A stack of cassette tapes, their cases cracked like windshields, crowded the stereo. Posters of Jimi Hendrix and Run D.M.C. covered a juvenile's illustrated sports-themed wallpaper. Mostly balls. The twin bed was unmade and grey sheeted. Golden plastic trophies on faux-woodgrain bases crowded the child's two-drawer desk, from which flakes of orange paint peeled. Little league, school athletic competition awards. A single window had even been installed, covered by a roll-up blind designed to hide the fact that the window offered a view of nothing but an interior wall. A few beanbags leaking birdseed white stuffing camped in front of a small television hooked to a first-generation Nintendo Entertainment System. Overhead a single sixty-watt bulb shone wanly.

"My whole empire, all tha shit, it started right here. Now I want ya'll to feel me: Before *everything* came the dream. That's what you got to recognize. My vision began right here, and it's where it begins to this day."

Shaun turned in a circle with his palms up. He looked at the woman he was paying to put on my arm up and down.

"What's your name, honey?"

"Asia."

"Ooo, I *like* that," he said. "Think you find your way back out of here?" Asia nodded. "Go on then, sweet thing. Maybe I'll get with you later. Men here have some business to transact."

Major coughed.

"Oh, my bad," Shaun said. He extended his hand to Randi.

"Must be the suit, Mr. Braun," Randi said.

"Naw, it ain't," Shaun said. "Ya'll follow me."

You wouldn't know by looking at Shaun D. Braun that he was a celebrated NFL superstar. He was compact, muscular, but didn't carry the lineman's bulk around. He did not look like a gladiator. He would never have a nickname based on the shape of appliances. He opened the bedroom's narrow closet door and stepped into the dark mass of ill-fitting coats and dunes of destroyed sneakers.

"Watch your step now," he called back as he receded further into the closet. I had almost lost sight of him when a crack of light appeared in the darkness and a door opened on the other end of the closet, where the back wall should have been. It turned out that the replica of his childhood room was merely an antechamber, the closet a tunnel.

"Problem is, players in this game forget where they come from. Forget that fire to rise up, you feel me?"

The room on the other side of Shaun's closet resembled a cross between a comfortable salon and a lecture hall. From the floor level ascended three tiers of home theatre chairs, five chairs a piece. At the head of the high-ceilinged room stood a podium with a gavel and microphone. Behind the podium hovered a medium sized movie screen flanked by two brown, velvet curtains. Love seats and lounge chairs lay at odd angles facing the podium. Shaun took his place behind the podium and motioned for us to take up positions on the ground floor level of living room furniture. Shaun picked up the gavel and cracked it against the podium, though the room was completely silent.

"Love that shit," he said, looking at the gavel. "Ever since I was a kid, watching *People's Court?* Wapner come down on that gavel, people come to attention, right? All right, let's get to it. 'Bout six months ago, I'm at practice and I'm thinking how this game ain't gonna last forever. Hot as shit, sweating, running drills. I start thinking: Shay-D, what you gonna do when this game's done? What's gonna take you to the next level. Now I got my boy Clooney say, 'D.D.B., you'd be right for this script,' and on the flip side, I got people sayin' 'Shay, look what Fiddy did with that Vitamin Water, hundred mil, baby.' But in my gut, deep down, I know it's just part of the same game, you feel me?"

"I certainly do feel you," Pontius said. Shaun glared at Pontius like he'd discovered a turd in the cocoa puffs. He looked at Major.

Major leaned over and whispered, "Don't say *shit* until he bangs the gavel again."

"Now where the fuck was I? Major?"

"The game," Major said and cleared his throat. "All a part of the same game."

Shaun clapped his hands together, "Right. Now I'm sweatin', feel my whole body on fire. I see it all unfold, like a holy vision. All the same game. It's all the same game, Shay-D. And like, I don't know, something come over me. I pass out right there on the field. And that's when it hit me. I heard a voice, this fine ass voice in my ear, like you'd hear in the club when some honeys up on you for that private dance. And feel me, what you think that voice said?" Shaun banged the gavel and pointed it at Randi.

"Play the game harder?"

"No." He pointed the gavel at Pontius.

"Wake up?"

"What? No." He pointed the gavel at me.

"It's all the same game?"

"Naw, but I like that you listening Slim Jim," he banged the gavel. "The voice says: *Reinvent the game, Shay-D.*" Shaun leaned into the microphone and whispered. "Re. In. Vent. Tha. Game."

Shaun paused for dramatic effect and folded his deck-rope forearms across his chest. "Then the voice is gone, and it's like my eyes are open, but you know, they still closed, and it's like I'm looking into the sun. And I'm thinking: That's some deep shit. And: How do you side step the game? The game is *all.* The game is what this shit is founded on. You either winning it or losing. And my brain's boiling. Then I see, coming out of the sun, this tiny speck. And it gets larger, and I see the speck got legs, and then I realize this thing coming out of the sun is coming for me."

Shaun banged the gavel and pointed at Randi.

"What was it?"

Randi stammered. "The game master?"

"The who? Naw, naw."

"An angel?" Pontius said.

"Mmmmnaw, not specific enough."

"A message from God," I said.

"Could be, Slim Jim, could be. But not what I was thinking on. What it *was* was a golden chariot. Drawn by a team of the most deep, snarling-ass pit bulls. Like, the hounds of Hell rose up and jacked that chariot from Heaven to bring me this message. But feel it, ya'll... the chariot ain't got a driver. The spot is empty, it's just these crazy pit bulls coming down. And I realize right then: Shay-D, *you* the driver. They bringing you your *destiny*. These are your *dogs*."

We were all still completely in the dark as to why we were sitting in Shaun D. Braun's court, but he seemed to think that the lightbulbs would begin glowing for each of us. Randi had her concerned squint on, the one she used when pretending to think deeply. Pontius was nodding his head, though slowly, as it became clear that Shaun physically intimidated him, and he was afraid any quick movement might attract Shaun's attention. I was beginning to wonder if Sadie could get her hands on a second bomb jacket my size.

"I can see by the looks on ya'lls faces that you coming to the same conclusion I did," Shaun said. "Don't look so busted, Major. I told you this was money." Major's face was a toothless grin which communicated simultaneously, *Guess you got me, Shaun* and: *Shaun, you dumb motherfucker*.

Shaun directed his attention to the back of the room, to an unseen person behind the controls of the media room.

"Yo, Pookie! Roll tha DVD!"

Nothing happened. A thick cloud of marijuana smoke billowed out of the small, square window in the back of the room.

"POOKIE! ROLL! THA! D! V! D!"

The room faded to black and a thumping, stuttering, syncopated beat began at bowel-loosening volume. The screen flickered. At first, it seemed as though we were watching an out-of-focus home video of a ballet, but as the hand shot stabilized, it became apparent we were watching footage of a real dog fight. In slow motion, the pit bulls scratched and snapped. Sampled barks added a counter rhythm to the main bass line. A human voice imitating growling noises joined the fray. A montage of bloodied and snarling hounds paraded by as the beat thundered down on us. Shaun D. Braun's profile was visible in the light cast from the flat screen so large I had mistaken it for a projection screen, and he was popping his fist into his palm and nodding along with the beat. Just as quickly as it began, it ended in a big-metal-vault-slamming-shut noise, and four letters faded up through the darkness: F N D F L.

"Lights, Pookie!" The lights returned. "Props to Pookie, he threw that shit down in iMovie." We joined Shaun in a bewildered round of golf claps. A second cloud of smoke rose to the ceiling from Pookie's invisible blunt. Major Washington's chin rested heavily in his hand, his face deflated.

"What ya'll just seen is the future. The new game. And I'mma own it." Shaun banged his gavel and stepped down from the podium.

"FNDFL?" Randi asked.

"First National Dog Fighting League, baby! Whole world ready for this shit. It's the next level. I'm done playin' on the field, I'm ready to look down from the box. What you see right here before you is the One True President of the First National Dog Fighting League."

"Ah," Pontius began, at first tentatively. "Well. You know. Some of our nation's top intellectuals have begun to compare professional football to dog fighting. Malcolm Gladwell, for instance. It's a discussion that's out there, to be sure."

"See?" Shaun pointed at Major. "What'd I tell you? Uhn! Time is *come*." He clapped his hands together once.

It was just the encouragement Pontius needed.

"Yes, Mr. Braun, it's an ancient story. A battle of honor. It represents the true heart of man manifest in his most loyal friend. You *could* argue that all of sports history has been moving towards this *inevitable apex.*" Randi looked at Pontius, and Pontius smiled at her with the come-along-with-me-now smile I'd received when Pontius needed back-up to keep from sounding desperate for the money. It was an art form, the seamless tag team in the pitch. The treacle thick counsel glazing the lips of the black-hearted advisors.

"Walls *are* coming down," Randi started, rummaging in her jargon bag. "Distinctions between sports and violence paradigms are realigning. Timing is imperative in these convergences. You could own the conversation around dog fighting. Lead the conversation, in fact."

"I couldn't agree *more*. Easily bigger than the NFL, NBA, and Major League Baseball combined," Pontius said. "It's all very preliminary, of course, but in a time of war, the position for this brand could evoke themes of intense loyalty, family, the ultimate sacrifice. I'm detecting notes of *victory to come*, even. Dare I say a glimpse of eternal peace? When our human differences can be settled in canine combat. Our noble, four-footed warriors."

"Tha invisible apex," Shaun said, his index fingers steepled on his chin. "That's dope. Ya'll is sharp for a bunch of country-club looking motherfuckers. How 'bout you, Slim Jim? What do you make of the new game?"

I could feel the motives of three different parties bearing down from behind poker faces.

"Considering everything I've seen—especially this year—" I said, leaning forward in my seat, "America's more than ready for this. You might even say we're all hungry for it. Commissioner."

Major Washington's eyebrows nearly jumped off his forehead.

"Oooo! Commissioner!" Shaun clapped. "Aw, shit!" He sprung up in the air and turned a circle, the intimations of an end zone dance. "That's right! That's what I like to hear! You *my boy*, Slim Jim."

My boy. A line from a story my father used to teach ran through my head. *That's the best position they is.* I sat in on his classes at times, the days when I entertained the life for myself, the precocious professor's son slouching in the back row, getting the gospel that it mattered. I could see him behind his own podium, his glasses flashing, the chalk dust on his blazer. Grammar undone in the line drive of the bullet. *That's the best position they is.*

Chapter 12

In Which We Witness How Defeat Is Snatched From the Slobbering Jaws of Victory

Shaun D. Braun had built a small arena in a building behind his mansion where he held the weekly dog fights that later became so famous in the news. This was the building where the party raged, the smaller pirate ship in the shadows of Shaun's house, his career, his public image. Unlike the house, this building emitted no light and the only windows were stationed high under the eaves like lookouts in a pillbox bunker. The two-story building, constructed of utilitarian concrete block concrete, looked like a garage for agricultural machinery. A single backhoe stood sentry at the border of the abandoned fernery beyond the building. As CNN would later report, beneath this field, the bodies of a few hundred dogs decayed in hasty mass graves.

We entered through the rear, the team assigned to elevate the Commissioner's First National Dog Fighting League to national prominence. The staging kennel was just inside the door, presumably so the evening's gamblers could get a look at the dogs before they decided how to lay their money. There were pit bulls, Rottweilers, and mutts of fearsome but indeterminate bloodlines. Handlers, who more often than not resembled their dogs, stood by like little league fathers at the fence line, tough-faced with churning stomachs.

There were black dogs and piebald dogs, cropped ears and missing eyes. Some panted, some sniffed the blood in the air. Others scratched at their cage doors, the muscled humps of their shoulders levitating charged hair. Weapons were carried openly in the kennel. Jumper cables coiled in the corner behind the door, a fresh green truck battery nestled in the center.

Shaun escorted us past the kennels, the owners deferential to him when he stopped to push his fingers through the mesh of a cage. Varieties of his nicknames were murmured. Behind heavy double doors an amplified voice rode above a wash of shouting men and heavy music. Everything smelled of shit and blood and laced blunt smoke and raw sweat and celebrity cologne. The noise behind rose and broke in waves.

Suddenly one of the doors burst open and a full-bearded man of about three hundred pounds charged through carrying a meaty and mangled mass. He cradled the dying dog in his arms and shouldered through the back door. A gunshot followed shortly after the back door slammed shut. Randi concentrated on her BlackBerry.

"Ya'll want to pick a soldier now?" Shaun asked. "I play my gut when I see 'em in the corners, but to each his own, know what I'm sayin'?"

"As the commissioner goes, we go," Pontius said. Luckily Shaun hadn't heard him.

We entered in the lull between fights. At the center of the arena itself was a hard packed circle of Georgia clay and white crushed shell. Concentric rings of freshly poured concrete bleachers flanked the ring, packed with spectators shouting at one another, into cell phones, and to a few bet makers who stood ringside with the handlers. Bright white spots deified the ring. A hump-backed Mexican man raked the blood into the clay and dirt with a wide, wooden-tined rake. The DJ lorded over all from a plywood skybox isolated in a corner of the arena, and by his side an MC looked down on the action in the ring. All around cash changed hands.

Men licked their thumbs and whipped through hundred dollar bills, smacking stacks against the backs of their ringed knuckles. Above the ring, on the opposite side of the entrance, an empty section of the bleachers remained cordoned off by purple rope on brass corner posts. When the MC spotted Shaun enter the arena, he nudged the DJ and grabbed the microphone to announce Shaun's entrance over a beat. Once situated in our VIP box behind the ropes, Shaun took a wireless mic from the DJ and stood in the center of the ring.

"Ya'll here for a special night. Tonight we start to take this game to the next level. The peoples you see right here in the VIP box," here Shaun pointed the microphone at us, staring from our box like so many of the dogs in the kennel cages. "They got the plan to take this shit right here international."

Some shouts rose up from the bleachers, but you could tell that a good number of Shaun's crowd felt the same way Major Washington did about Shaun's vision for the First National Dog Fighting League. The handlers for the next round clutched their dogs by the scruff.

"Now before we kick this round off, I'mma turn the mic over to the man in charge of making this shit happen."

Pontius began to stand, holding his jacket against his belly.

"Slim Jim, get the fuck down here and tell 'em how we gonna make it real."

I didn't process "Slim Jim" as my name until Pontius flopped back onto his concrete seat and shot me his upper-lip-to-dry-teeth smile.

It was the last thing I saw before the power was cut.

The raid on Shaun D. Braun's property was coordinated by a task force consisting of representatives from the FBI, ATF, and the Fulton County Sheriff's department. Had there not been a dick measuring contest between the Fulton County SWAT and ATF agents, we probably wouldn't have had the time to flee the arena and pick our way through the dewy, snake-infested fernery on the hinterlands of Shaun D. Braunworld. The newspapers later cited this when criticized that the number of arrests associated with Shaun D. Braun's death kennels was unacceptably low. Someone cut power before the argument of who would be first through the door was settled, and at that point, the handlers in the kennel unpinned the cages, and hell was quite literally unleashed. The dogs set on the very next thing through the door, which happened to be Fulton County SWAT.

I became separated from Pontius and Randi in the fray. With the power out, the stars were visible again. A helicopter swept the property, but I was deep into the fernery, hoping that I didn't feel the fang of a pygmy rattlesnake through my sopping Hickey Freeman pants. I passed over fresh mounds of dirt, some torn open by scavengers, and the smell of roadkill wafted up from where the rotting dogs had been picked over by raccoons. I stumbled into pits where things wormed.

A popcorn noise sounded in the quiet after the helicopter banked and carved a wider circle. Some of Shaun's guests exchanged gunfire with ATF from an upstairs window. I looked back only once, when I felt I was far enough away. It looked like a ship going down in fits and flashes.

I remembered my BlackBerry after I'd been on the lam for what felt like an hour. It was missing from my belt. I wound my way in the dark between the bony pines of a thin wood. The temperature dropped, and as I walked through the scrub, a low fog bearded the needled floor. Despite being alone and freezing, I was relieved that I hadn't had to take the microphone from Shaun D. Braun and lay out our master strategy for promoting dog fighting to the national stage. Because I would have tried. Within twelve hours, the media would solve this problem, though. Somewhere between cell towers, the voices of Major Washington and Randi's husband, D.B., floated, plotting the plays far into Shaun's future.

I crab crawled up an embankment and surfaced alongside a two-lane blue highway. Its pavement buckled and cracked under the weight of its own idleness. I could see the ribbon rolling far overland under the blue-white moon. I rested on the shoulder and listened to my own breathing. Thirty thousand feet up I traced the red and white lights of a passenger jet. I hung my head between my knees and listened to the insects.

One creaking bug noise rose over the rest. It grew louder. I looked up the road and saw the black shape of something moving steadily towards me. It was my father in his wheelchair. I stuck my thumb out hitchhiker style.

"Gas, grass, or ass, son. No one rides for free." He parked himself next to me and pulled the little lever of his wheel brake.

"Why am I less and less surprised to see you?" I stood up and wiped my hands on my ruined suit pants.

"What's the next adventure for the knight errant and his stubby Sancho Panza?"

"This isn't the last one?" I asked.

"You tell me. I'm not the one who keeps charging the windmills, am I?"

"Yeah, well, it's not like I have a choice in the matter."

"Oh, what terrible free will you have! The problem is you have too many choices. You think there's someone up there running your show down here? You want no choices, you try being dead."

"Why is it you're hell bent on telling me I'm alone in the universe?"

"Why is it you refuse to listen?"

"You think I didn't get the message growing up?"

"Save it for the crowd, Camus." He waggled his thumbs over his shoulders. "Start pushing."

"I hope you're all entertained on the afterlife channel." I took my position behind his wheelchair and grasped the black rubber grips. I could feel their cheap ridges press into my palm, and it was a comfort. "Got a divine GPS on this thing? Which direction is the closest gas station?"

"You know what they say. If you find yourself going through Hell, keep going. Pick a direction and stick to it. The only way out is through."

I thought I could hear dogs barking all the way from Shaun's kennels. It had been a long time since I'd been completely unwired and in the weeds. I looked up and down the road for a sign or the glow of a gas station beyond a rise. I snaked him one way, then the other. He stuck out his arms and made airplane noises. *Reeearrw, wrreeuuuuhn.*

One way appeared to slope downhill before climbing again. The other climbed immediately. Uphill seemed right. I pushed my father down the yellow center line. We followed the road for a while not speaking. No cars passed, no headlights disturbed the moonlight. We crested the rise in the road and a small lake spread out in a depression a few hundred yards off of the road, like a black mirror sunk in the weeds. We stopped to look at it.

"We used to fish," I said.

My father looked out at the lake, his hands folded in his lap.

"You mean we used to sit in a canoe."

"True. Most of the time. But not *all* of the time. Do you remember that trip we found that hole in Luke's Pond? It was almost dark, but we tossed a last cast into a pocket of lily pads—"

"And they bit. Boy did they bite. Just kept biting."

"Every cast, a fish. I'll never forget it."

"You were eleven," he said. "Probably the worst thing that could have happened."

"We always fished catch and release. Just kept bringing in the fish and letting them go."

"Ruined you for good. You thought it would be that way every time we paddled out in that damned canoe. Fish on the line every time. We had to be catching the same fish over again."

"It was pitch dark when we decided to leave. We paddled around that lake a long time," I said.

"It felt like half the night. My shoulders still ache to talk about it. You were shitting your pants, if I recall."

"You weren't, though, were you?"

"Of course I was. If we tipped the canoe… anything could have happened. It's the little lapses in attention that kill you. They add up."

It was so still you could almost hear the bass break the surface of the lake, hunting insects.

"I remember I was scared of the dark, but I wasn't afraid we'd die, I don't think. I wasn't afraid we wouldn't find our way home eventually."

"You should have been," he said. "You think I got a secret grown-up club card when you were born? Don't you know by now that fathers are large children?"

"No guardian angels, then."

He shook his head slowly. "Not that I've seen. Oh, that reminds me. You dropped this."

He reached into his slacks and pulled my BlackBerry out, its red eye an unnatural star.

"Of all the things reincarnated," I said.

My father snorted. "I wouldn't bank on your bonus round if I were you."

The white beams and orange running lights of a semi truck broke over the rise in the road far behind us. My father didn't turn his head to meet the light. He looked down the grass valley to the black lake. It was the first time during any of our encounters I thought he looked like a corpse. He edged his wheelchair off the concrete and onto the clay shoulder. He rolled himself forward slowly, and the wheelchair seemed to lock onto a hard-packed path hidden in the high, dry grasses. He moved further down the path the direction of the lake, the grasses rising over the wheels, over the handles, over his shoulders. Soon he was just a rustle in the weeds, indistinguishable from a slim breeze combing the country.

I hailed the big rig with the BlackBerry's bright white screen. I waved it in the air slowly to and fro like a lantern.

Chapter 13

The Great LaBar Partners Limited Retreat,
Or: A Little Fiddling While Atlanta Burns

Without the proof of a ruined suit and a platinum VIP bracelet still locked to my wrist, I would have thought the previous night's events at Shaun D. Braun's party another complicated nightmare in the periodically broken chain of waking nightmares which constituted my life. As I remember it, the trucker dropped me at a service station near the interstate and I was able to call a taxi on the immortal BlackBerry.

After four A.M. I limped into the Atlantan Terrace lobby, where even the whores dozed in the threadbare chairs, their heads tossed back and mouths fixed in the perpetual "O" of their inflatable counterparts. My feet were blistered, my pants crusty with dried clay, and my eyes felt like sea salt marbles. I had finally reached parity with the grand dame that served as my home away from home. I didn't sleep as much as I ceased to exist for five hours.

I clicked on the television. Cable news headlines in Atlanta centered on the raid of Shaun D. Braun's kennels. I caught a glimpse of our rented Bentley secured behind yellow police tape, and thought about the stroke Mackie Wallace would have when she realized LaBar

Partners Limited had effectively purchased the luxury rental through federal seizure. Agents deposited Shaun into a black Crown Vic. He was wearing the same clothes he had been wearing while holding forth behind Pookie's podium.

The last remaining question was if Pontius and Randi had escaped arrest, or if they were protesting their accommodations in a Fulton County holding cell. Beside the bed, the Blackberry's red cyclops guarded the answer. I preserved the fantasy they'd been arrested and called Sadie in San Francisco. I'd forgotten the time difference, though, and her sleepy voice picked up.

"You can't do this thing you're planning," I said.

"Where are you?" she asked.

"Atlanta."

She sighed in my ear.

"You can't do this thing, because—" On the screen Shaun D. Braun looked out of the back window of the Crown Vic and into my eyes.

"Because why," she said, her voice half in dream.

"Because I need you. And… I want to get married and have kids and—"

"No you don't, Nick," she laughed. "You need to stop saying the things you think people want to hear."

Ok. I didn't want to get married or have kids, as far as I knew.

"You know what I can do now?" she asked. I could hear the phone sliding against the comforter and pillow case. All I wanted at that moment was to be there with her, and yet I was lying naked on a top sheet wearing a Tiffany bracelet from a dog fighting party hosted by an NFL superstar.

"What can you do?"

"I can turn on a lamp with my iPod."

"So you're saying we have remote control lamps?"

"No, Nick. I'm saying I can light things up." She yawned.

The stillness on the line was total. Darkness in the fiber optic thread.

"Wait for me. I'm going to be home soon," I said, not knowing if this was true. "Don't strand me in Atlanta."

More darkness.

"Everything here is breaking apart."

Was I talking to myself? I heard her one sleep-rolling noise and then nothing. She'd passed out. I'd be nothing but her dream today, as she was mine. I was in love with a suicide bomber. I was talking to the ghost of my father in bathrooms and moonlit fields. I was in the employ of demons. Who had put these people in my life? Who had put me in my life? Who was holding me in my life?

I walked to the window and opened the blinds and all around was the green canopy of Atlanta's suburbs, punctuated at intervals by fast food restaurants and supermarkets and strip malls. The Atlantan Terrace, being an old hotel with cheap owners, still had windows that opened. I opened one as wide as I could and leaned my torso over the edge into the cold wind against the 14th floor. The brushed aluminum sky hid jets threading the dense clouds.

What terrible free will you have! I heard my father say. I stepped back from the window and gathered up my ruined suit. I threw it out the window and into the draft, where it unfurled for a moment in the perfect form of a falling man before jacket and pants parted ways. I squeezed my hand and worked the bracelet over my fist, scraping blood from my knuckles. I winged it through the blank window like a frisbee, the sound of its landing too far away to hear.

I had my second suit out ready for departure when someone knocked at the door. I wrapped myself in the bed sheet and looked through the peephole.

It was Randi Bevelecazzo, fresh as ever.

"Nick! Are you in there? Nick?"

I cracked the door, keeping the burglar bar in place. Randi waited in the hallway gazing into her BlackBerry.

"So you made it out last night. Did P.J.?"

She held up her finger *wait a second.*

"Did you lose your BlackBerry? We're having the retreat today. It's been moved up. I need you to coordinate food procurement with Mackie Wallace. Get dressed and check your email."

She walked away from the door and I lost sight of her. I opened the door and stepped into the hallway in my sheet.

"I'm not coming!" I shouted. "Count me out! I quit!"

I heard her footsteps stop on the marble floors before the elevator.

"You can't quit, Nick. I'll see you on the roof at noon."

The roof?

To: LaBar Partners Limited <execs@labarpartnerslimited.com>
From: Pontius J. LaBar <pjlabar@labarpartnerslimited.com>
Subject: RETREAT TODAY

In the wake of last evening's significant setback with regards to our flagship client, I have made an executive decision to hasten the arrival and shorten the duration of our scheduled retreat.

All staff shall meet at noon today for an emergency strategic planning session on the roof garden of the Atlantan Terrace Hotel in Midtown. I will arrive separately, shortly after noon.

Professional attire only! A picnic lunch will be served, but the event will be BYOB (Bring Your Own Beverage). Refrain from alcohol prior to or during the retreat, as we will require the utmost clarity and your very best ideas.

Let us gather to briefly celebrate our victories and recommit to surmounting our challenges. I am convinced this will be a morale boosting event.

Rally, team! Lead the charge! Canard shall not see our sunset yet!

Ever onward!

The temperature in Atlanta dropped in only the way the onset of a winter storm in the southeast can herald. The morning began as warm as it would be all day, and the cold blustered along on hard-blown Canadian winds. Dressed in my spared second suit, I stood with Mackie Wallace in the greasy humidity of *Chickin' Xpress ATL*, waiting in line to place the order for the retreat's picnic food. The joint—earning the title in full freedom from irony—was wallpapered with Coca-Cola advertisements gone gold and black with fryer residue. The staff and patrons were almost entirely black, with the cooks wearing hairnets instead of ridiculous paper caps.

Randi Bevelecazzo had left us to handle the prep work for the retreat while she fit in a deep tissue massage to alleviate the stress of last night's fugitive hours. It was not clear to me how Pontius and Randi avoided arrest, though it was possible they hid and then blended in with the field of FBI suits that had descended on the place when the power returned. She pretended it did not happen while her husband and Major Washington eagerly soaked up the gravy of damage control.

"How much chicken are we talking about here?" I asked Mackie. I noticed that she had a peculiar new streak of white hair I presumed to be Bentley-inspired.

"Twelve buckets, plus sides."

"Twelve buckets? There's going to be… what… you, me, Pontius, Randi, Ono?"

"And Chet."

"Chet's *back*? Wow. I never thought I'd see him again. You must be relieved he's safe."

Mackie's smile revealed equal gum and tooth. "They sent him back when the invoices were past due."

"Two buckets of chicken each?"

"Mr. LaBar wants to ensure the feeling of abundance."

The cashier, a mountainous black woman with two inch glitter nails, cocked her head with four hundred years of indifference as a sign she was ready for our order. Mackie withdrew her BlackBerry from its holster and read from the screen. As she listed the food, the cashier produced low frequencies acknowledging each item.

"Three large mac and cheese, two collard greens, two large cornbreads, two large coleslaws, ah, and twelve buckets of mixed chicken, fried, and two gallons of sweet tea."

The register beeped and clicked with the cashier's nails.

"You want that for here or to go?"

Mackie made a disgusted noise not unlike Pontius' own indignant squeal. "Are you serious? Does it *sound* like it's for here? Am I really going to sit down and eat *twelve buckets of chicken?*"

The cashier's head snapped up and unhinged itself in an orbit around her shoulders. *"Bitch,* I don't *know* your life!"

We walked into the wind, lugging sawed-off cardboard boxes stacked with chicken buckets and steaming sides. The entrance to the roof of the Atlantan Terrace was at the top of a narrow service stairway. The wall of the staircase featured a large arrow accompanied by the word POOL painted in red. Whatever elevator had once lifted guests to the roof was long abandoned. The passageway paint peeled and the air smelled of mold.

On the roof, a gusty gray sky and the dismal skeleton of a pool party which had ended some time in the 1950s. Weathered aluminum lounge furniture with sagging green-and-white vinyl supports crowded the edges of the concrete deck. The deck itself was patched many times over with rivers of roofing tar. Circular iron tables lay staked through with steel poles that may have once been topped with canvas umbrella sunflowers. All was raw metal and the absence of comfort. The centerpiece of the deck was the kidney shaped swimming pool, drained. Brown high-water marks from the previous decades of rain and periodic snow formed age rings within the chipped concrete bowl. A brick wall at knee height was the only demarkation between the deck and a sixteen story plunge.

Ono fruitlessly attempted to tamp down paper picnic tablecloths with masking tape. Her chihuahua barked and nipped at the flapping paper. The orchid centerpieces tipped over, spilling their water on the deck. Chet Wallace hovered at the far corner of the roof looking like a boiled down chicken carcass. He wore an eye patch with a thick pad of yellowed gauze beneath. After some loosely coordinated tussling presided over by Randi's managerial oversight, we managed to fashion a sad buffet near the brick wall. Someone had carried up a trove of decaying metal folding chairs, so we arranged them near the tables, fearing at every turn that we would inadvertently contract tetanus. It was a far cry from the Reynold's Plantation resort brochure that had been eagerly forwarded earlier in the year.

We waited for Pontius.

By one o'clock, the glistening grease within the valleys and mountains of the fried chicken congealed white in the cold air. Chet Wallace meandered his way to the buffet and took a scoop full of mac and cheese in his fist and ate it out of his hand.

No word from Pontius.

Close to one-thirty, the noise of a helicopter caught our attention. It circled the rooftop two times before hovering above the flats opposite the empty pool. When it became clear that the helicopter meant to land on the roof, we all took cover towards the buffet. The rotor wash hurled three buckets of chicken over the edge of the brick wall. Fried chicken parts rained on the passersby of Midtown.

It settled tentatively, dragonfly-like. The helicopter door rocked open and Pontius lurched down. He turned and waited, arms outstretched. The helicopter's rotors lashed all with storm winds. Gradually, the fire-orange fur ball that was Shelby tumbled out onto the deck, nearly knocking Pontius to his ass. The orangutan clapped his hands and stomped in response to the helicopter's furious whupping.

Passengers shat, the pilot picked up his bird whirled away, no doubt mystified why he had just chauffeured an old orangutan and a suited handler to the roof of the Atlantan Terrace. Shelby charged Ono's chihuahua as though the little dog was a long-lost child of the jungle tribe.

"Unacceptable!" was the first word shouted from Pontius' mouth.

Ono wrung her hands as Shelby curled the chihuahua in his arm and nestled him against his prodigious throat pouch. He waddled to the buffet and fished a chicken thigh from the bucket, stuffed it in his mouth, and then pulled out some of the partially chewed meat to feed Ono's chihuahua. The chihuahua inhaled the meat and licked Shelby's fingers.

"How do you expect us to conduct high-level planning in this setting?" Pontius railed. "Honestly, am I the only one who *thinks* anymore? We're facing dire days for this firm. Canard has once again robbed us of prosperity. We narrowly escaped with our lives and *this* is how you prepare to save your jobs?"

Pontius hiked up his suit pants and approached Shelby.

"No, Shelby, no! Put the doggie down."

Shelby bared his teeth and humped around the rim of the empty pool, putting good distance between himself and Pontius.

"Shelby!" Pontius circled the pool, but Shelby matched his stride. They orbited the deformed nucleus.

"Chet! Go around the other way. Cut him off," Pontius barked. Chet didn't look up from the buffet. He had a beard of coleslaw running over his chin and onto his shirt. It was not entirely clear that he could hear at all.

Pontius huffed, his face pink. "Ono, get your goddamned dog."

The two closed in on Shelby. He protected the chihuahua. Pontius reached to lift the chihuahua from Shelby's grip. That's when the dog snapped at Pontius' hand, possibly expecting an oily piece of chicken. No matter, the damage was done. Pontius squealed as the dog's tiny razor teeth sunk into the fleshy mound between thumb and index finger. The cry startled Shelby so bad that he loosened his grip on the chihuahua. Pontius flailed with the little dog lock-jawed on his hand. Ono shouted, Shelby snarled, and in one furious flourish, Pontius pitched the chihuahua over the brick wall and off of the roof.

There was possibly only a few seconds of total shock, but it felt much longer. It was as if a howling wind that had been blowing for two hours suddenly ceased and took our breath with it. Ono collapsed onto the deck. Shelby charged Pontius and rammed him into the deep end of the empty pool, where he crumpled.

A lot of what happened after that comes in wild snatches of image and sound, none of which synchronize. It happens in a strobe light.

Shelby suspended in the air, lips flared, lunging into the pool after Pontius.

A savage screaming mingled with snorts and a general wetness.

Randi's brown leather handbag disappearing into the stairwell.

Mackie Wallace hurling cold chicken pieces at Shelby.

Chet Wallace looming over the rim of the deep end with a greasy grin upon his death's head.

The police report records that responding officers had little choice but to shoot the orangutan, given that he let no one approach as Pontius lay bitten, broken, and bleeding in the bottom of the empty pool. They fired two shots, one of which missed and ricocheted into Pontius' exposed left buttock. The other, however, struck Shelby through the chest, shredding his aorta.

The report does not record his mournful, expiring hoot.

Though he had lost a lot of blood, broken his arm and his jaw, and had multiple bite wounds on his lower extremities, trunk, and face, Pontius did not die at the bottom of the pool, as his constant companion did. The paramedics back boarded him like a bloody rare roast and air lifted him to a trauma unit. He departed in the same ostentatious style as he had arrived, though considerably worse for the wear. Ono had to be sedated.

The police took my statement and released me. I wandered out of the Atlantan Terrace for the last time, picking a path through flocks of pigeons tearing at smashed chicken parts.

Chapter 14

The Death Throes of the Empire & the Emptying of Paradise

For a time, it was a vacation. No one emailed, no one called. A month passed. A final paycheck appeared in my account. Then one morning the BlackBerry stopped blinking. I felt a tremendous stillness from the east, as though Pontius J. LaBar's acolytes had disbanded and receded into the clerk and cubicle nothingness from which they spawned. I half expected to see Randi Bevelecazzo at my door, though, calling me back to Atlanta, requesting I book a flight to Cleveland, St. Louis, Atlanta, Philadelphia. So, in a sense, it was not a vacation, but the anxious escape of a boy skipping school for the first time.

Good news had come for Jake Hawkins, and he was offered a residency at Amherst, where he would write and teach poetry. We spent a day drinking whiskey in the park, lounging on the lawn of the Conservatory of Flowers and listening to the drummers on the other side of the trees. Grown men played whiffle ball like boys. The cast of characters from the Lone Palm shifted in and out of our day, congratulating and hating Jake for his good fortune. I chartered one last limo to the airport to see him off, and the screeners at the security checkpoint gave him shit as he passed through the gate as a passenger for the first time. I turned my back on the airport, relieved not to be a traveler, but anxious to see him go.

All in all, the timing could not have been better, as Sadie and I were notified by the leasing manager of the Tantamount Building that the mighty black AMEX had been declined. We had a few days to vacate, most of which we spent listing and selling the apartment furniture on Craigslist. The props in the play were removed one by one. Strangers came and took the set pieces away until the stage with its incomparable view of the city was bare.

Sadie and I retreated to the pigsty on Hayes, among the clouds of Lily's BBQ smoke and the wheat paste murals peeking from trash bin alleys. It felt right. Sagamore greeted us with his great brown skull and swayback nag posture. Jake had kept my old room like an abbey. We saved one of the white Eames' chairs, but it looked ridiculous among the shabby cast-offs and a little ominous as well, like the seat the poltergeist commands, a gateway which could permit the demons to emerge again. We sold it off.

I was aware the money had come to an end. The engines were off. They wouldn't kick back on. We were on the glide path. It was a time of letting go.

On a clear February night, we carried a cardboard box with us to the Golden Gate Bridge inside of Sadie's duffel bag. We'd packed the last artifacts of my involvement with LaBar Partners Limited—the stillborn BlackBerry, business cards, the impotent AMEX—and pitched them over the edge into the cold bay far below. It was an unsatisfying ceremony, spreading the remains as we did. It felt disingenuous, as though I'd picked the easiest symbolic act to avoid a harder task, something that would require more of me than an ocean and gravity.

Sadie and I walked back to the bus stop rather than cross the bridge. I had tried to put Sadie's mission out of my mind. The blue parka lined with plastic explosives was neatly folded in a trunk in my closet on Hayes. Somewhere I had intermingled her mission with my job at LaBar Partners, making the mistake of believing that when I escaped, she would also be free.

We stood side-by-side and faced the bridge while listening for the bus. The great persimmon steel spanned the water in a gold halogen cloud.

"I have to go away," she said. I pretended not to hear. She withdrew a small glinting object from her duffel bag. "Take this."

In her hand was a silver clamshell phone.

"It's disposable," she said. "Pre-paid. So, you know, I can let you in on how I'm doing."

"You're changing your mind."

"No. But it was easier to focus when you traveled all the time. I have to go away."

"You should follow that first instinct, the one where you're finding it hard to focus because I'm here."

Why did her smile always make me feel like the child? As if I had made the child's request. I remembered her sitting in the lobby of *Purv*, paging through her electronics magazine. I pocketed the phone.

"I have to finish," she said.

"No you don't. You don't have to do this at all."

"I do. I know you don't understand it. Maybe you will someday."

A white National Park Police cruiser pulled into he parking lot and slowed to scan the cars. Sadie looped her arms around me and buried her face in my chest. I instinctively put my hand on her back, unsure if she was drying her eyes or hiding her face. The cruiser swam its shark circle and disappeared beneath the dark underpass. I clutched her as though I could absorb her body into mine, wishing desperately to fold her matter into my matter. A lone man walked up the ramp to cross the bridge, and I wondered if he'd come here to quietly disappear halfway.

"So is suicide a family tradition?"

She tried to pull back, but I held her tighter. "Is it genetic? Is that what you're telling me?"

She thrashed hard. I let her go. She backed away and shouldered her duffel bag. I hadn't thought twice about the duffel bag when we'd left the house, but I realized then that the jacket, the iPod detonator, the whole works were probably in the bottom of it. I had nothing left to play, so I played desperately.

"Your brother didn't die from any roadside bomb. He was a prison guard. And he shot himself."

She put down the duffel bag and took one step closer. Now I was on the other side. Now I was the enemy.

She stopped and folded her arms over her chest. "I know this. You know this. So what?"

"So maybe you can cut the shit and start dealing with your grief about it."

"Dealing with grief! Is that what you're good at? Really? Is that what you've been doing so well?"

She was case-hardened, a bunker buster, accustomed to falling.

"This is what you do with grief, Nick," she lifted the bag off the curb with one hand and shook it. "You build something."

"You build something... to kill innocent people?"

"Who's innocent? Everyone's complicit. People get hurt with or without your help. You build."

"It's thin, Sadie."

"No, you asshole, it's everything."

The MUNI bus swung into the lot, lit from inside like a rolling aquarium, the shadow of a few people inside. I raised my arm in case the driver missed us standing by. When I turned around, Sadie was further away from me, her duffel bag strapped over her shoulders.

"Come on," I said. "Come back home with me. I'm sorry I said anything."

She backed up the ramp a few paces. The bus slumped at the stop with a hiss. She knew I wouldn't leave, so she left, and I watched her leave.

The driver called out. "Hey man, you getting on or not?"

On the bus I stared through my damp reflection into the warbling, streaking chaos of taxi crown lights. Somewhere in the darkness of the Marina, the bus heaved to a curb and kneeled for a wheelchair passenger. The ramp unfolded, and a big man swathed in scarves and a 49ers knit cap guided his motorized chair into the space behind the driver. I had expected to see my father roll into the aisle. I wanted him to appear.

I wondered if I hated Pontius LaBar not because of what he represented, but that he had built something and I had not. Had I preferred to become an agent in that which I hated rather than risk failure? My father had taught, had ignited himself in a classroom and sent the students into the world, fragmented with new ideas. But I was again where I had begun, and the people I had known over the past year were now carrying on in their trajectories, our alignment had been temporary.

I rode along in the bus until I felt it was part of the problem, the riding along. I pulled the cable and got out at the next stop. It was the first decision in a chain of decisions.

I walked all the way up Divisadero from the Marina. The first time I saw the backside of Divisadero's epic hill was at night, from the back of a taxi, and I mistook the streetlights rising up the hill for the lights of a tall office building far in the distance. It reminded me of the other high places you could get perspective on the city, how at height you could not see the streets running between the narrow houses. San Francisco was a place of illusions, a city drawn on God's Etch-a-Sketch, waiting for one earthquake to shake it out. Sadie's disappearing act felt like the first tremor.

When I made it back to the Hayes house, Sagamore did not greet me at the foot of the stairs leading up to our floor. The house was still. I called him, but I didn't hear his tags. In the kitchen, his food and water bowls were full. I heard the Hayes 21 bus woo-and-crackle along its electric wires and checked the living room.

"It's a funny thing, son. I never see dogs in the afterlife, and I think it's a bad sign."

My father's wheelchair sat beside our undertaker's couch. He stroked Sagamore's head. Sagamore panted, his long ribs shivering.

"I think: No dogs? This must be Hell. But maybe it's a species thing. Dogs go one way, people another. Or maybe the dogs are running the show."

"How did you get up the stairs?"

"You're very troubled by the insignificant," my father said. "Supernatural communication you take at face value, and you ask me how I got up the steps."

"I'm unemployed again," I said. "Sadie left me."

"Sagamore, look who's here! Droopy Dog. There are his favorite words: 'I' and 'me'. He never, ever, ever gets tired of them."

Sagamore's eyebrows cocked back and forth between me and my father.

"You're telling me you've given up? That you quit?"

"We had a dog, if I remember correctly."

"Poor son of a bitch," my father said.

"Correct me here if I'm wrong, but I recall he was a gift to you from one of your students," I said. "What was her name?"

"Who can remember? Details. She wasn't important."

"Well, I bet you remember the dog's name."

"Sebastian. A regal dog."

"That's right, Sebastian. A purebred Golden Retriever. We kept him outside, all by himself in the backyard."

"You going somewhere with this?"

"You tell me."

"O.K. I'll hazard a guess. Let me finish the Woeful Tale of Poor Sebastian. We took that dog to stud, and the bastard died mid-deed. The weak heart of the purebred!"

"Abandonment anxiety."

"Yes, son, I hear you loud and clear."

"And mom said 'No more dogs.'"

"And there were no more dogs. But let me remind you: I also buried that dog. I picked up his stiff body, wrapped him in a black garbage bag, dug the hole in a driving rain, and put him in myself."

"Tell me again about the driving rain?"

"More or less. It was sort of muddy."

Sagamore hoisted himself up and shook his ears. His chain rattled. He slinked off the couch one leg at a time and trotted to the kitchen.

"There we go," my father said. "Back up and at 'em." He dusted his hands off on his navy slacks, cuffs hanging footless at the minor fore wheels of his chair.

"Here's what I can tell you, son. When you're digging a hole with everything you've got, you forget about yourself, your little troubles. It's the same with all work."

"Digging holes. Nice."

"Maybe not all work. If you can find it."

My father hoisted himself sideways into the chair and wheeled himself down the hallway to the kitchen. I listened to Sagamore chew dry dog food. Eventually Sagamore wandered out alone and rubbed his side against my leg. I scratched his hind and found his leash and took him out to transact his business.

Chapter 15

Resignation on The LaBar Family Farm

In the best of fairy tales, the frogs become princes again and the wicked are punished. The bad things that have happened are undone and what has troubled us along the way teaches us. The ghosts go free, the princesses are married, and the kingdom is restored. The shoe cobbler does not remain the shoe cobbler. I see your ever and raise you an after. As it should be. We earned it. We showed up. The restoration of order is permanent.

Permanent, at least, until such time as the franchise storytellers decide a sequel would be too lucrative to pass up, and an executive someone writes a memo to a producer someone and wonders if a little ordinary magic might be cast, and they start sniffing around for that one new hot shot a couple of kingdoms over, the one who wrote that blockbuster last year? And yes, the evil dark lords were sealed in their crypts for all eternity, and yes, yes, but if you think about it, eternal peace was just *implied* wasn't it? And so the witches' agent gets the call, and the voice of the frog will probably beat the DUI, and if not, well, maybe the frog's brother shows up?

Pretty soon, the forces of evil get a second shot, and it works. The bards knew it would work, because they knew we were all a little sad when order was restored in the first place. A little bored to think about the prince and princess ruling the kingdom in perpetuity.

I think it was Joni Mitchell who rhymed "figure skater" with "coffee percolator" to more or less make this point.

And the shoe cobbler does not remain the shoe cobbler for long.

I was flying on my own dime to Florida. I had errands to run.

In *SkyMall* magazine I studied an ad for a solar-powered jerky maker. *Beef, wild turkey, gator, venison! The Woodsman's Natural Pantry, only $49.95. Never pay grocery store prices for dried meat snacks again!*

Bing.

"Ladies and gentlemen, as we make our final approach into Orlando International Airport, we ask that you bring your seat backs and tray tables to their full and upright position. Flight attendants will be by shortly to collect any cups, newspapers, or other items you wish to dispose of, and make sure your seat belts are fastened low and tight across your lap. Now is also the time to turn off and stow those portable electronic devices. Welcome to Orlando."

People forget they built the Magic Kingdom on swamps.

The morning after my father appeared in the living room on Hayes street, I called Atlanta-area hospitals to find out what had happened to Pontius. I learned nothing of his specific condition, but I did find he was transferred to a hospital in south Florida—Tampa, in fact. From there, a clerk in admissions indicated he had been released. When Pontius had been P.J., a student of my father, he had gone home on holidays to family in South Florida.

It was a two-and-a-half hour drive from St. John's Landing into the hot palmetto and grove country. I reasoned I could find him there, however reluctant he was to convalesce in his childhood home. Where else would he go? He couldn't afford to pay the royal court anymore, and so it was back to the country where the myth of himself did not exist. I picked up Interstate 4 from the Orlando airport and pointed the rental car south.

I found the address for the LaBars through public land records online. A five-digit number on a "county road," one of those addresses that locals mark by its distance from a single blinking light over an intersection with a Jiffy Mart. Beyond the interstate, the landscape unfolded into broad tracts of agricultural land, mostly flat and peppered with cattle. Groups of twenty and thirty plastic and steel mailboxes hung nailed to creosote-weeping railroad ties.

Having gone so far south and west, the rental car's GPS sing-songed me east, the sharp little triangle that represented my car blipping into territory where the roads abandoned names for numbers. A wrong turn at the crossroads represented a half-hour or more of back tracking. Flatbed, pig-nose big rigs pushed shockwaves of humid Florida air.

At a convenience store the color of a dirty tube sock, I stopped for gas. Prepay, cash only. Beside the register sat a two-foot high jar of pink pigs' feet in vinegar. The thin wailing of an inconsolable pop-country cowboy wheedled at a woman departed. Plump, rusty hot dogs rolled through infinity on a stainless steel ferris wheel cooker behind the counter. At the gas pump, a truck with wheels as high as my waist pulled up. In its rear window, a yellow sticker: TERRORIST HUNTING PERMIT NO. 9-11.

I checked my disposable cell phone. No calls, no texts. No Sadie at all. I'd left a note at the Hayes street house, just in case. I scrawled flight information, the number at my mother's house, and left the door to my bedroom unlocked.

The terrain turned to shallow rolling hills, and the GPS produced an alarming noise that signaled I was on my own.

Recalibrating. Recalibrating. Recalibrating.

The triangle sailed from the road's green line into black space, scout in a 2D universe. A single dirt road met the edge of the blacktop, white sand spreading onto the paved surface like the delta silt of the Mississippi.

Irrigation ditches flanked the road. I was profoundly glad not to be driving here at night. At infrequent intervals, a house or trailer clung to the swell of a hill. Most looked abandoned. I came to a second dirt road which met the one I was on at a perpendicular angle. On a stout fence post, a flayed plywood sign adorned with black and white mail-box letters read: LABAR FARMS.

I turned in. A metal cow catcher rumbled under the tires. The road pitched an elbow curve and screwed through an orange grove gone to seed. Some trees had run wild, others were stubby and scoliot-ic. High grass silvered the furrows between each untended row. Some sickly fruit clung to the branches, weighing them low. Rotten citrus caved in on itself. I startled an armadillo as I crested a rise in the road, and it scuttled for the undergrowth, gunmetal back shivering.

The LaBar homestead, a white clapboard two-story ordered out of an early Sears catalog, loomed over a muddy depression which may have once been a pond. The house itself leaned slightly forward, and the pump house and tractor barn did the same. It looked as if they would all one day converge on the pond. A green and white Ford F-150 from the early 1980s guarded the barn. Its front wheels were gone, the windshield a nicotine yellow. To the house's original construction a wide front porch with an aluminum roof had been added, supported by raw four-by-four beams. A fringe of leathery fly strips hung at inter-vals. I parked the rental car in a patch of sand which suggested a well-worn parking space.

The air was still and hot and there were no animals on the farm as far as I could see. I turned back to the house to find a woman scarcely wider than the posts holding up the porch staring down at me, smoking a cigarette. I raised my hand in greeting.

"I thought all the nurses had given up. You here from the home care agency?" she called out.

"No," I said. I stood at the bottom of the porch stairs. "My name is Nick Bray. I'm an associate of P.J.'s. An employee, actually."

She rotated her jaw as if tasting what I'd just said. Smoke leaked from each orbit.

"He doesn't have any money for you. If he ever had any at all."

"So he's here? I'm not here about money. I just want to talk with him."

"I'm Gracie," she said. "P.J.'s mother. You gonna stand there and wait for the sinkhole to catch you, or are you gonna come inside?"

I waited while Gracie LaBar served me iced tea in the parlor. Pontius was asleep in the "library," a room towards the back of the house closed off by pocket doors. The place was Murphy Oil clean and smelled of old pianos, brittle fabrics, and cigarettes. The windows admitted some white light through the warped panes, but the interior remained in a state of twilight.

Ornate rugs, antiquated furniture, and framed photographs choked the space. It was so dense, so layered, that the effect was that of a kind of nostalgic pine bark growing layer over layer inside the house. It seemed that the photos were hung over paintings which were, in turn, nailed through tapestries and flocked wallpaper. It was not hard to see why the LaBar Partners' offices were spare cubes of glass and light. A heavy swinging door lead to the kitchen, and behind the parlor couch, a narrow staircase ascended to hotter elevations.

In a medium sized oval frame above a collection of vases and tarnished candlestick holders, a fading color photograph showed a picture of a young boy on the shoulders of a tan man in a white undershirt. The man's head was bent down and against it the boy balanced a steel pail filled with fat oranges. The boy reached up into the branches of a nearby orange tree. Though the boy was shirtless and thin, his moon-shaped head and dark walnut hair was unmistakably that of young Pontius.

Gracie returned from the kitchen carrying a tray of Saltines and a block of Velveeta cheese half sprung from its foil. The tea was so saturated with sugar that crystals whirled among the ice.

"Is this P.J.'s father?"

She snorted. "God no, that's one of the Mexicans we kept on the farm. Back when it was a farm. P.J.'s daddy liked to safari."

"Safari?"

"That's what they call it when you go killing things in Africa, isn't it? He spent every dime doing it. Barely had the bills paid before he spent a bushel on his next adventure. I got a whole bunch of stuffed animals in the barn if you're looking to buy."

"Did P.J. ever go on safari?"

Gracie laughed her way into a wet cough. She cleared her throat, spit into her napkin and lit a fresh cigarette. The ringing of a bell sounded from down the hallway.

"I miss the Mexicans," she sighed. The bell rang furiously. Gracie did not seem to hear it. The ring turned into the sound of someone beating a bell against an end table.

"Sounds like my baby boy's up. If you're here to talk, by all means." She raised her iced tea in the air as if toasting me, and I wondered if her tea had a little more Southern Comfort than I enjoyed.

By the time I reached the end of the hallway, the banging bell had ceased. I slid open the pocket door and a flood of light spilled into the hallway. The room was at least ten degrees hotter than the rest of the house, and large rectangular windows framed by heavy maroon drapes covered the three angled walls. When my eyes adjusted, I made out a hospital bed with its back to the center window. Instead of facing the tortured orange grove, the bed faced the wall, of which the pocket door occupied a small corner. The room had to be as high as the second story of the house, and it was clear by the architecture that the room had also been added on some years after the house's original construction, presumably by Pontius' father.

I did not immediately recognize Pontius impacted into the mattress. He didn't have his glasses on, and his time in the hospital had taken at least twenty pounds off his frame. His face was a field of lemon yellows and plum bruises. Owing to some surgery, what hair there had been on his head had been razored down to nil and was growing back around furrows of scars. One of his eyes remained covered with a gauze bandage, just as Chet's had when he returned to the roof of the Atlantan Terrace. The servants' bell he'd been thrashing lay discarded on the floor beneath a portable toilet on a metal frame. Judging by the smell in the room, it could use emptying. His hand flopped on an adjustable table, feeling about for his glasses.

I approached the side of the bed, and took his glasses in my hand. He made a few guttural noises. His jaw was wired shut. He looked fearful and defiant, like a car-struck dog. He breathed heavily through his teeth, one of which was broken into a knife edge. His lips were whitecap chapped. His one eye locked on me, but he could not see my face.

"P.J., it's Nick." His eye roved. "Nick Bray."

I placed his glasses in his hand and he pushed them on, hand shaking. His breathing calmed.

"Nick," he said, his clenched jaw pinching my name.

"Yeah, it's me. Surprise."

Pontius stared at the wall opposite the windows while he calmed down, and for a minute or so I stood there in the way people do in hospitals when it's clear that all of the platitudes will fall short of the pitiful, viscerally vulnerable condition. I had stood this way at my father's hospital bed a number of times. I remembered the way the casts bulged like fat, white match heads over his freshly amputated legs, when he was hallucinating on a gratuitous cocktail of morphine and oxycontin.

Pontius stared at the far wall. From floor to ceiling the wall was covered with photographs and the taxidermied heads of animals—tusked boars, gazelles, cheetahs. They were sun faded and losing their hair in patches. A handful of bleached white skulls hung at the highest level, presiding over the room with ivory antlers and yellow teeth. In the center of the wall was an enlarged photograph in black and white of a man standing among a grassland collection of giraffes.

One in profile looked identical to the LaBar Partners Limited logo. Head lifted in an almost arrogant attitude. I stepped closer to the wall of trophies. The man among the giraffes was smiling, but his eyes were shaded. The photo was a poor enlargement, the print itself assaulted by the Florida sunlight. The man was a smudge and shadow.

"Your father, isn't it." I said.

He grunted. "Ny uhr you here?"

"I'm here because I needed to see you."

Pontius snorted. "Ny buthur?"

"I came to resign."

I looked at him in his bed, and having said it, I didn't feel any better. He did not betray a thing. Had I expected him to? It was possible I had come to see him suffering, but in seeing him suffer, I was unsatisfied.

"I needed to tell you face to face."

"Cuhnrd," he mumbled. "Muz cuhnrd ull uhlong."

"No, it was not Canard. Canard did not put you here. You put you here, and that is all."

"Iz nut uvurh yet." The white in the corners of his mouth cracked. "Cuhnrd—"

"Shut up! Enough already! They don't exist!"

That was when I realized why I had come, and why I was still angry. I had come for authenticity. I was angry that he had shown no sign of regret, no sign of honesty. No admission of reality, no break in the fantasy. That even ape-bitten, butt shot, broken and one-eyed, he still had the resolve to hold his teeth tight in his delusion. His lips were set in a line.

"You wasted your talent," I said. "And you had it once. My father saw it. And you wasted it."

He raised his eyebrows.

"You squandered your life. Squandered it on—on intellectualized prostitution."

He lowered his chin and smiled tightly to himself.

"You chose to waste it."

He sighed. "So you kit."

"I am. I do. I quit."

Pontius did not say another word. He leaned up in his hospital bed and took a pen and a piece of paper from his side table. Turning his head to focus his one good eye, he wrote slowly and deliberately. Finished, he folded the paper in half, and then half again, and held it in the air. I took it, but did not give him the satisfaction of reading it in front of him.

He removed his glasses and placed them aside. He closed his one eye. I ceased to exist for Pontius J. LaBar.

Twenty minutes down the road, I realized I still had the note pressed in my palm, mashed against the steering wheel. I shook it open. The blue ink had bled from my sweat, and some of the letters had inked my palm. The note said:

WHAT EVER YOU DO WITH YOUR LIFE
I WILL BE THE REASON YOU DO IT.

RESIGNATION ACCEPTED.
PONTIUS J. LABAR

It was not the first time he had heard the things I'd said to him. I had said nothing original. He had smiled because *I thought* it was the first time he'd heard them. Just like that, I was written out of the script.

Chapter 16

Guidelines for Transporting the Deceased

The Transportation Security Administration provides specific guidelines when traveling with crematory remains:

Passengers are allowed to carry a crematory container as part of their carry-on luggage, but the container must pass through the X-ray machine. If the container is made of a material that generates an opaque image and prevents the security screener from clearly being able to see what is inside, then the container cannot be allowed through the security checkpoint. Out of respect to the deceased and their family and friends, under no circumstances will a screener open the container even if the passenger requests this be done. You may transport the urn as checked baggage provided that it is successfully screened. We will screen the urn for explosive materials/devices using a variety of techniques.

After my trip to the LaBar family farm, I drove north and stayed the night in St. John's Landing at my mother's house. I told my mother that I thought it might be nice to scatter my father's ashes from the

Golden Gate Bridge, but this was just a story to get the old man's dust out the door. I wasn't sure why I wanted him or what I would do with him, but it seemed like a necessary thing, or at least a thing that shouldn't be left unresolved. I had one of those B-film notions that scattering his ashes would stop his supernatural visits. But did I claim the ashes to stop the visitations, or was I afraid my mother would toss them and I'd never see him again? I did not tell her I'd barely had a moments rest from him in the year since he'd died.

In a broken sleep I dreamt I let him go from the jet at altitude.

I left before dawn for my flight, the cardboard box lined with the plastic sack of ashes. A ground-hugging white fog nuzzled against the headlights on the drive to Orlando. At the toll plazas, flashing yellow lamps emerged long before the booths. I passed through three toll gates, pitching silver change into the machines' upturned mouths.

I deposited Dr. Michael W. Bray's cardboard box in the plastic tray with my pre-paid cell phone and belt and sent him into the X-ray machine at Orlando International Airport. He sailed through the black rubber curtain. *See you on the other side.* We boarded the terminal train under white neon arcs. Its electric motors hurled us towards the sleeping jets, tethered and whale-like.

I strapped my father's ashes to the top of my roller bag and wandered the cavernous Southwest terminal. The shops booted slowly, the whole airport gradually coming online. Red, sun-roasted kids trailed behind their parents with Sausage Egg McMuffins stuffed in their fists, Mickey Mouse ears still fragrant with the sweat of yesterday in the parks.

Attention! This is an important announcement from the Department of Homeland Security. The nation's current threat level is at ORANGE.

A boy asked what it meant and his father said to be on the lookout for men with long beards and white towels on their head. The father laughed and un-boxed four orders of hash browns into a pile on waxy yellow paper. They worked the ketchup packets in their teeth. I was given the idea to cut a hole in my father's ash box and sprinkle a peppery benediction on their breakfast. Or I could change flights for a layover in Las Vegas to dust the Golden Nugget with his immolated remains. A little in the trays, a little on the tables. A little in the carpet and a little in the air.

Or I could just be done with it.

I tugged my luggage into the handicap stall and cut open the tape sealing the cremains box. There he was, bagged like a dirty drug, white and black and star-flecked with fragments unnameable. I lifted the plastic sack out of the box and held it over the toilet bowl. I listened. Someone dragged a roller bag into the bathroom and stowed their luggage in an adjoining stall. The stall frame rattled as they closed and latched the door. I thumbed the heat-sealed lip of the bag and tugged it lightly to see how easily it would give. I heard no wheelchair, no vaudevillian rhythm pulsing under his breath, no cha-cha-cha of dancing stumps. If he had any supernatural fear of washing down the john, he was calling my bluff. I boxed him up and refastened his box to my bag.

In the terminal, the televisions all turned on at once and shouted CNN a hundred milliseconds out of phase.

I checked the time on the throw-away clamshell phone. 6:18AM. To my surprise, I had missed a call from Sadie. In security? Last night? The number was blocked, but the voicemail's envelope icon winked. I plugged my open ear to block out the televisions and concentrated on her message.

"Hey there… Nick." She sounded thick with a cold or drunk. There was a long pause. Rustling, pacing. The electronic beep-beep of the BART train in the background preceded a howling rush of white noise. "So I didn't want to—" Her voice was lost in the train. "—and so I stopped by your house. Sagamore was glad to see me. I read your note. Looks like you're coming home… tomorrow?… which I guess is today for you now. I'm O.K. I don't think my number shows up on your phone, but if it does, don't bother calling me back." The robotic BART voice announced: *TENCAR-DUB-BLIN-PLEZUNTUN-TRAIN-ARRIVINGIN-TWO-MINUTES PLATFORM ONE.* I could feel the electrically charged air of the underground station. "I hope you're happier, that you got to see your Mom, or whatever it was you were up to in Florida. How about this. I'll meet you at the airport after you land. Come down to baggage claim. So I can see you." She sighed long and heavy and her breath passing over the microphone distorted the sound. She did sound lit. I could make out a second BART train arriving in the background. "I'm going to lose you—"

The voice mail ended in the banshee wail of the BART train.

Definitely drinking. I wished that Jake Hawkins had not left San Francisco. Wished that he was still there, as he had been when I was traveling all those months. Wished he would be at the airport.

CNN persisted. A reporter in a red tie and black overcoat interviewed a seven-year-old girl who sold artisanal lemonade on her Williamsburg stoop for $6 a cup. Her fraternal twin DJ'd these events. Their father had purchased him two Japanese turntables and taught him. A scruffy someone postulated child street chefs were the new food carts. The father was also writing a blog-to-become-book on this subject.

After this news, and a lot of news like it, a Southwest gate agent told us to line up against the wall by letter and number. This reminded me both of grade school recess and preambles to ethnic cleansing.

We boarded the plane and I placed my father in an available overhead bin. I had always wondered, when she'd wired up the bomb jacket and the detonator and knew how to work it, and felt she'd finished her last tattoo, what would make any one day more special than the next to carry it all off, to put those tools to use?

How do you pick the date to complete the mission? Do you pick one people can invest with meaning, as with the gape-mouth nine and two towering ones? Or do you pick a private date, one that will give a forensic psychologist a little *aha!* as he mines your life's artifacts?

Dear diary: Today I watched TV.

Dear diary: Today my whole world was destroyed.

Dear diary: Today.

Do you pick a homecoming? A homecoming missed?

Down the jetway we all walked in line, thinking of which seats we'd claim for ourselves. Surely the Germans had a word for the simultaneous feeling of ecstatic anticipation and black terror flooding one's heart. Maybe it was an American word we hadn't invented yet.

The flight attendant asked me to turn off and stow my cell phone. All the stowing. I didn't realize I was staring at it. I turned it off and pushed it into my pocket. Nothing but five and a half heavy hours, a window seat, and the free verse of SkyMall Magazine.

Our flight attendants made silent signals to one another up and down the aisle. They began the FAA prayer, and we all enjoyed our petty freedom to ignore it.

There are six exits on this Boeing 737 aircraft.

Take a moment to locate the exit closest to your row.

Here is the sturdy aluminum buckle that will save your life when the engines shear through the cabin.

Here is the tray table that may kill you, so it must be upright and locked.

Please note that the nearest exit may be behind you.

I woke up in light turbulence over the Rocky Mountain foothills. A guy of about my age, possibly younger, sat in the aisle seat of my exit row, writing on a yellow legal pad. The plane bounced a few more times, and the fasten seatbelt light dinged on. I remembered the first time my father appeared in the forward lavatory. The turbulence battered away, and my row mate gave up his writing and capped his black pen.

Far below us, the mountains were still flocked white with the winter snow packs. He crooned his neck to look out the window, so I leaned back. The plane took a hard drop and the passengers made the involuntary roller coaster whoop that they sometimes do. The aisle guy looked anxious.

"There's always turbulence about now," I said. "It's the mountains. You come to find it reassuring. It means you only have two and a half hours or so to go."

He looked familiar. Or I found people who looked uneasy to be familiar.

"I don't fly much."

"Lucky you. Flying out for a job interview or something?"

"No. I'm thinking of moving to San Francisco."

"You aren't originally from New York, are you?"

"No?"

"Just saying, save yourself the trouble and stay in New York. There are a lot of people who come to San Francisco just to talk about moving back to New York."

"You from New York?"

"No, Florida. Originally."

"Yeah? And you live in San Francisco now?" He turned towards me in his seat, as though I'd just materialized fully for him. This, I recognized. Here was someone thinking about gambling everything. Without knowing the particulars of his life, his face summed up all of the curiosity. I was someone who had made the leap.

"How long ago?" he asked.

"Three—no, four. Four years now."

"You had work, though."

"No, no work. I just moved. I needed to move. I was a runner. Long story."

This information didn't seem to hearten him, this idea that it was possible to start over with next to nothing in a city like San Francisco. It was almost as if he had been looking for the exception that proved the rule of my surviving the transition. That he might be looking for an out, a rational reason to undermine a risk he had to take.

"I'm Nick, by the way," I extended my hand.

"Eric."

The plane bucked and fell a hundred or so feet and we could feel the extra gravity as the pilot pushed the plane to try a higher altitude. The engines sung a higher register.

"So no job and you're thinking of moving. Mind me asking why?"

"I met someone. Someone I think I might need to move out to San Francisco to be with."

"Man or a woman?"

"What?"

"A man. Or. A woman. They did ask you, didn't they? Your friends, family. It's a Florida thing. Word a young man sets off alone for San Francisco… eyebrows up go, pretty soon—"

"Soap jokes." He smirked.

"Soap jokes. Don't drop the soap."

"A woman, for what it's worth."

"Either way. Good enough reason. Better love than money," I said.

His faced changed, a flash of ready defense suddenly checked, maybe thinking he had to defend whether or not it was love, whether or not it was too soon to say. The plane settled into smoother air. I wondered if my father's box would tumble out of the shaken overhead bin when I went to retrieve him.

"Do you go back to Florida a lot?" he asked.

"Just this once in the past year. Well, twice. This was the first time I'd been back in a year."

"Family? Business?"

"Kind of a mix. I needed to pick up my father's ashes."

"Oh." He was embarrassed. "Sorry to hear that."

"Don't be. I mean, thank you, but don't be. It was over a year ago that he died." I pointed up. "He's riding along in the bin above 12C. I've got some time off now."

I liked that he didn't say anything else. That he didn't say *it must be hard*. Or *I lost a dog once*. Or *wow, a whole year? What have you been waiting for?*

"I was thinking about taking the... BART train? But I don't know... Do you maybe want to split a taxi? After we land? "

"She's not meeting you at the airport? This someone you've flown three thousand miles to see?"

He tapped his pen on the legal pad. "It's a surprise."

The conversation had lulled me away from my own life, but the word *surprise* brought Sadie's face into tight focus. He must have sensed me tense up.

"Hey, don't worry about the taxi... I should probably figure out the train anyway."

"No, it's just that someone might be meeting me. You should definitely take a taxi if it's your first time. Not that you'll get lost on the train. But you should really see it from a taxi the first time. You should start getting your eyes used to the place. You won't believe it for a while."

He didn't seem to understand, but he seemed like the kind who would eventually. It had not been that long, but it was hard to remember clearly what it was like to take it all in for the first time. Maybe that's what he was writing, why he was writing. So he wouldn't forget.

"I'll let you get back to your note pad," I said.

The fasten seatbelt light dinged dark and we were free again to move about the cabin. We slipped back into our individual traveler's reverie. My window, his scribbling.

I woke up when the wheels hit runway 28R.

What If I didn't deplane? If I held onto the seat, my peanuts, my flotation device.

We taxied. There was no continuing service, and they would force me off eventually. The ground crew waved us in with their orange wands. I did not want to let go of the suspension of my life. I could buy another ticket and preserve it, but only for hours. Air travel is the world between worlds, the passing of time only for distance's sake. I had hated it, felt acutely the expulsion from the city each month.

But now we had landed, and now I had to see what was left. We stood, my seat mate and I, hunched under the overhead bins, and watched as those ahead deplaned, bobbing and catching, gathering artifacts of themselves, leaving waste. Eric went, and I went, and I pulled Dr. Michael W. Bray off the shelf and tucked him in the crook of my arm.

The forward motion was compulsory.. We flowed into the terminal and joined the river of people rushing towards their lives again. I lost sight of Eric.

It was a bright, clear morning in San Francisco. The hard, white, optimistic light of the west coast morning flooded the airport. Back east, they'd been grinding at it for three hours, but the west thrummed like it had just invented the day. While this side of the country stirred in its last dreams, I had been traveling back in time, reclaiming our hours spent from the forgiveness of time zones.

We arrived in a torrential influx of Monday morning traffic. The terminal smelled of jet exhaust and burning coffee. No ground holds, no pattern delays. Good visibility. April and no midwestern storms. Men leaned into gate agents and wheedled for upgrades. Among strangers, I recognized myself in a dozen past incarnations at a dozen gates, but now that time had passed.

The lines at the security checkpoints wound back and forth, a coiled mob among the shouting of TSA screeners and the hard noise of trays smacking stainless steel rollers. Eighteen cameras I could see pointed their barrels down at us. The crowd texted urgently before their devices were passed one time through the X-ray machines. Two or three whole planes' worth of impatience, grinding against a small platoon of white-shirted screeners. I instinctively looked for Jake Hawkins, though I knew better. He was good and gone, breaking his lines in Amherst, and I was glad for his safety in his stanzas. I passed through the no-return checkpoint, the exit point through which one becomes unclean.

Baggage claim lay below. The escalator's horizon vanished and renewed itself. Arrivals stepped on the escalator and it ferried them down, bodies and carry-on baggage sinking. A second escalator, mostly empty, brought people from baggage claim to the security checkpoint. My father's ashes sloped awkwardly against my side. I stopped to fasten them again to the roller bag.

I joined the down escalator. I wanted to see Sadie again, and I hoped not to see her here. I had the fever of a sick kid, afraid to see the angel at his bedroom window, for what she signified.

Hark.

She was off to the side, half hidden behind two chauffeurs holding signs for their arriving clients. She was as invisible as she had planned, a young woman listening to her iPod, the blue jacket a hue between the dirty sky carpet and pale blue pillars of the baggage claim's low ceiling. I wanted to approach her, to embrace her. But I recognized the jacket.

That blue-bird-of-happiness parka was the same one she had modeled for me in the Tantamount apartment, the night of Jake Hawkins' reading at The Lone Palm.

Now it was time to leave the nest.

These were the minutes to be viewed and reviewed in the months to come on security tapes.

She met my eyes briefly and picked up her cell phone. I did the same, expecting it to ring. She unhooked the white headphone from her ear and walked towards me, at the same time paying no attention to my presence. She stood close by, not greeting me, the two of us standing in proximity with no connection, only our phones held to our heads like a dozen other people dazed in the blue shifting fluorescent lights.

"I'm taking off soon," I heard her say into her phone, though the words were chosen for me, and not the phantom on the other line. "I just wanted to get in touch while I still could."

It was hard not to turn towards her.

"We've had a lot of conversations like this," I said, staring into the monitors above the luggage carousels. I could smell her perfume, I was that close. Jasmine amok.

"You should take a taxi," she said.

"To tell you the truth, I'd like to split one. Maybe I could convince some lonesome girl down here to change her mind about her travel plans."

"It's a perfect day to fly," she said.

"No time for coffee before this trip?"

"I'm pretty wired up already," she said, her voice not so steady.

"That's not funny."

Everyone on their phone stared into middle distance of their missing companions. I took a few steps away and turned to gaze at Sadie's back. Her hand shook as it pressed the little burner phone to her ear. Her perfect ear. She did not turn to face me. She was protecting me.

They would be looking for any sign of anyone connected to her. I turned abruptly and gestured wildly over my head, as though engaged in some vital, futile plea.

"Fine," I said, a little louder than necessary. "I guess this is it." My heart struggled with my thick blood's pressure. "I love you. And I'll miss you. I'll miss seeing your face in the city."

"You're going to see my face everywhere," she said.

"I would do anything. Anything if you would change your mind about this."

"You'll be sick of me. I'm going to haunt you. They're going to haunt you with me. I love you, but you've got five minutes."

She shut her phone and slipped it in a pocket of the parka, presumably atop a pocket of roofing nails. I took one step after her. I said into my dead phone, "My love to your brother."

She put her earbud back in and withdrew the blocky old iPod from her jacket. She then seemed very still, so composed in herself. I followed her to the escalator leading to the security checkpoint above, just to carry the sweet smell of her in my head a few seconds longer. She stepped on and ascended. She glanced once down at me. I watched her rise. Soon, she was out of sight.

Five minutes.

Less than.

In less than five minutes a new story would begin.

In less than five minutes they would stop talking about kids in Brooklyn hocking lemonade.

In less than five minutes there would be a lot more signal and a lot less noise.

In less than five minutes the spectrum of the homeland security terrorist threat level would begin its red shift, as with all things moving away from us.

Taxis stacked on the departure line. I hustled. A few people waited ahead of me. One of them was Eric.

A Luxor Cab driver argued with the porter about something. A Yellow cab honked, and its driver popped out of his cab, ready to open his doors and snake the next run. A few tourists laden with bags waddled away from the porter to the Yellow cab.

Three minutes, maybe? Could it be down to two? The Luxor driver turned to see the Yellow cabbie loading luggage and charged to protest the stolen fare.

"Still up to split that cab?" I shouted to Eric above the noise. A third cabbie honked and the whole line erupted into a great bleating herd.

Eric did not recognize me for a moment, then his face brightened.

"Come on, let's grab one!"

We turned back to the choked line and I tossed open the back door of the first empty cab. The driver began to get out to help us with bags.

"No time!" I shouted. "Eric, get in."

He piled in. I tossed my father's box after, end over end, chucked my bag after, and swept into the smoky back seat. The cabbie looked over his shoulder and rocketed the cab around the altercation ahead of us. Porter whistles and angry horns. We left it all behind in a rush.

"Hayes and Broderick in the city," I said. The cabbie's bluetooth headset sparkled like a ruby in his ear, matching the numbers rising on his meter. The acceleration crushed us back into the seat. We merged with the 101 in twitches and lurches. The cabbie muttered into his bluetooth headset, the language muddy and urgent and gratefully unintelligible. Eric's attention drifted out of the window and across the water on the low stretch charging into Bayview. Candlestick stood on point like a tomb.

"Just wait until we come over the hill. The whole city will

unfold," I said to him.

Two highway patrol cars sped by southbound, lights flashing.

The cabbie's voice rose and died. His slender fingers pressed tight to his ear piece. A heavy fire truck lumbered after the highway patrol cars.

I asked Eric,"Where do you want the cab to drop you? Do you have an address?"

He rustled in his bag and looked on his legal pad. "It's... Carl and Cole?"

"That's not far from where I am. Hey man," I said to the driver. "Second stop—"

I leaned forward in the seat to tell the driver, but he held up his hand. His face was only marginally engaged in the road. The cab slowed its ceaseless acceleration, his foot slipped off the gas. He seemed to be asking a question again and again, as though the person on the other end was in the middle of a storm. I knew what it meant. Five minutes was up.

Sadie was already traveling along those early first-hand networks, flooding the ear pieces in Arabic, Vietnamese, Pashto, Urdu, Chinese, Spanish, a punctuation mark translated into a hundred languages, cascading in text messages and clipped dispatcher's voices. She had transcended her body and become media.

The driver found the gas. The taxi leaned under the Caesar Chavez overpass and swept up the hill, rocking us in our seats. Now would begin the journey backwards from safety to origin, from the terror to the birth of terror. Not long from now, it would be CNN or FOX or one of the infinite talking heads that would read from their teleprompter: FIRST DOMESTIC SUICIDE BOMBER.

Piece by piece, when they put her back together—the YouTube videos she left, the diaries, the email messages in limbo in her brother's account, his photo in uniform, the surveillance video outside a Motel 6 in Hayward where she met the vet who built her the jacket, the tattoo artists, the corporate no comments—I would get to know her again. How well she had hidden me, so well I would never be found. So that I didn't exist. So that I was given freedom when I should have possessed none. And so now this. And so.

"Oh," Eric said.

It was the view of The City, from the Bay Bridge to Sutro Tower, opened like a picture book below, majestic and sepulchral, colorful and at peace, teeming behind its still clock face. We descended.

"Worth the price of admission?" I asked. I rubbed my eyes and took a deep breath. "Worth writing about, right? You are a writer, right? The note pad, on the plane?"

"Working on it," Eric said.

"I've got to find something to work on myself."

We sunk below the city's skyline and banked hard left approaching the 9th street exit. This was the city where I would scatter my father's ashes, in its train tunnels and sidewalks and all of Sadie's favorite places. In her sun, in her parks. The cabbie chattered, his words speeding along with traffic.

"So Nick," Eric began. "What was it, exactly, you used to do?"

SIGNED THIS DAY, APRIL 4, 2012

Nicholas Bray, PRINCIPAL

R. Eric Raymond, WITNESS

Acknowledgments

My gratitude goes out to many for many reasons:
To my mother, Judy, of course, and my brother, Bryan.

To Kim Puckett and Ella Slinn, for their love, support, and endurance.

To Boyd Pearson, who was there, and Gina Hudson, who helped pull him out.

To the men of STS for Friday nights and tending to history.

To Matt Debenham for the decade of his support reading, editing, encouragement, and belief.

To my fellow travelers Mary-Kim Arnold, Lynne Carstarphen, John Cleary, Russell Dillon, Liz Hille, and Matt McGlincy.

To Scott Levitt and the Levitt Family for the generous financial support which made the writing of this book possible.

To the regulars at Reverie Cafe on Cole St. and the wildly kind family at Vierra & Friends on Carl St.

To the Bennington Writing Seminars, and my teachers Martha Cooley, Alice Mattison, David Gates, and Sheila Kohler.

To Blake Butler, for the retweet connecting me to Ken Baumann ("*Ever tried. Ever failed. No matter. Try again. Fail again. Fail better.*" "*No, you don't understand Mr. Beckett. Your card was declined.*")

To Ken Baumann, my editor and publisher at Sator Press, whose astonishing enthusiasm for every detail of this book went above and beyond.

To my father, Dr. Michael W. Raymond.

To all I cannot name.

To the City of San Francisco, the Infinite City.

Eric Raymond is a working writer in San Francisco. He was born in Daytona Beach and grew up in DeLand, Florida. He attended Stetson University in DeLand and the Bennington Writing Seminars in Bennington, Vermont. This is his first novel. He lives in the Cole Valley neighborhood with his wife, Kim, and daughter, Ella. Email him at eric@ericraymond.com or follow him on Twitter (@pontiuslabar).

free global brand management consultation at:

LaBarPartnersLimited.com